KENNETH GRAHAME'S

THE WIND
IN THE
WILLOWS

Illustrated by Eric Kincaid

INTRODUCTION

Kenneth Grahame's *The Wind in the Willows* was first published in 1908. It is easy to see why it has become one of the classics of children's literature and why it continues to appeal today. The characters are individual masterpieces; the setting of the English countryside shown in all its seasons is totally charming; the language is a combination of the poetic and humorous. *The Wind in the Willows* is a timeless tale that should be part of everyone's childhood.

In this edition the well-known children's book illustrator Eric Kincaid has fulfilled his lifelong ambition to illustrate *The Wind in the Willows*. He has brought a new dimension to the story with his delicate style, his eye for detail and his amusing touches. They add a fresh charm and make the story all the more enchanting to a younger age-group.

With the aim of making this delightful story more accessible to today's children, the text has been lightly abridged. Some of the most difficult words have been simplified and the longer sentences split for ease of reading and understanding. Three chapters from the original edition have been omitted. They are self-contained and in no way interrupt the sense or flow of the story. A further two chapters have been shortened and combined.

For those who already know *The Wind in the Willows*, this edition will be a visual delight to return to again and again. For those who are about to discover the world of Mole, Ratty, Toad and Badger for the first time, there is a double treat in store: a marvellous read, beautifully illustrated.

The Five Mile Press Pty Ltd
950 Stud Road, Rowville
Victoria 3178, Australia
Email: publishing@fivemile.com.au
Website: www.fivemile.com.au

First published by Brimax Books Ltd, 1986
This format first published 2005

This edition published in the UK by Brimax Publishing Ltd
Appledram Barns, Chichester, PO20 7EQ, UK

Printed in China

CONTENTS

CHAPTER 1
THE RIVER BANK

The Mole had been working very hard all the morning, spring-cleaning his little home. First with brooms, then with dusters; then on ladders and steps and chairs, with a brush and a pail of whitewash; till he had dust in his throat and eyes, and splashes of whitewash all over his black fur, and an aching back and weary arms. Spring was moving in the air above and in the earth below and around him, penetrating even his dark and lowly little house. It was small wonder, then, that he suddenly flung down his brush on the floor, said 'Bother!' and 'O blow!' and also 'Hang spring-cleaning!' and bolted out of the house without even waiting to put on his coat.

Something up above seemed to be calling him and he made for his steep little tunnel. He scraped and scratched and scrabbled and scrooged, and then he scrooged again and scrabbled and scratched and scraped, working busily with his little paws and muttering to himself, 'Up we go! Up we go!' till at last, pop! his snout came out into the sunlight, and he found himself rolling in the warm grass of a great meadow.

'This is fine!' he said to himself. 'This is better than whitewashing!' The sunshine struck hot on his fur, soft breezes caressed his heated brow, and after the peace of the underground home he had lived in so long the carol of happy birds fell on his dulled hearing almost like a shout. Jumping off all his four legs at once, in the joy of living and the delight of spring without its cleaning, he went on his way across the meadow till he reached the hedge on the further side.

It all seemed too good to be true. Hither and thither through the meadows he rambled busily, along the hedgerows, across the copses, finding everywhere birds building, flowers budding, leaves thrusting – everything happy, and progressive, and occupied.

He thought his happiness was complete when, as he wandered aimlessly along, suddenly he stood by the edge of a full-fed river. Never in his life had he seen a river before – this sleek, twisting, powerful animal, chasing and chuckling, gripping things with a gurgle and leaving them with a laugh, to fling itself on fresh playmates that shook themselves free, and were caught and held again. All was a-shake and a-shiver – glints and gleams and sparkles, rustle and swirl, chatter and bubble. The Mole was bewitched, entranced, fascinated. By the side of the river he trotted; and tired at last, he sat on the bank, while the river chattered on.

As he sat on the grass and looked across the river, a dark hole in the bank opposite, just above the water's edge, caught his eye, and dreamily he fell to considering what a nice snug dwelling-place it would make for an animal with few wants and fond of a riverside residence, above flood-level and away from noise and dust. As he gazed, something bright and small seemed to twinkle down in the heart of it, vanished, then twinkled once more like a tiny star. Then, as he looked, it winked at him, and so declared itself to be an eye; and a small face began gradually to grow up round it, like a frame round a picture.

A brown little face, with whiskers.

A grave round face, with the same twinkle in its eye that had first attracted his notice.

Small neat ears and thick silky hair.

It was the Water Rat!

Then the two animals stood and regarded each other cautiously.

'Hullo, Mole!' said the Water Rat.

'Hullo, Rat!' said the Mole.

'Would you like to come over?' asked the Rat presently.

'Oh, it's all very well to *talk*,' said the Mole, rather crossly, he being new to a river and riverside life and its ways.

The Rat said nothing, but stooped and unfastened a rope and hauled on it; then lightly stepped into a little boat which the Mole had not observed. It was painted blue outside and white within, and was just the size for two animals.

The Rat sculled smartly across and made fast. Then he held up his fore-paw as the Mole stepped gingerly down. 'Lean on that!' he said.

'Now then, step lively!' and the Mole to his surprise and rapture found himself actually seated in the stern of a real boat.

'This has been a wonderful day!' said he, as the Rat shoved off and took to the sculls again. 'Do you know, I've never been in a boat before in all my life.'

'What?' cried the Rat, open-mouthed. 'Never been in a – you never – well, I – what have you been doing, then?'

'Is it so nice as all that?' asked the Mole shyly.

'Nice? It's the *only* thing,' said the Water Rat solemnly, as he leant forward for his stroke. 'Believe me, my young friend, there is nothing – absolutely nothing – half so much worth doing as simply messing about in boats. Simply messing,' he went on dreamily: 'messing – about – in – boats; messing–'

'Look ahead, Rat!' cried the Mole suddenly.

It was too late. The boat struck the bank full tilt. The dreamer, the joyous oarsman, lay on his back at the bottom of the boat, his heels in the air.

'–about in boats – or *with* boats,' the Rat went on, picking himself up with a pleasant

'What's inside it?' asked the Mole, wriggling with curiosity.

'There's cold chicken inside it,' replied the Rat briefly; 'coldtonguecoldhamcoldbeefpickledgherkinssaladfrenchrollscresssandwichespottedmeatgingerbeerlemonadesodawater–'

'O stop, stop,' cried the Mole in ecstasies: 'This is too much!'

'Do you really think so?' inquired the Rat seriously. 'It's only what I always take on these little excursions; and the other animals are always telling me that I'm a mean beast and cut it *very* fine!'

'And you really live by the river? What a jolly life!'

'By it and with it and on it and in it,' said the Rat. 'It's brother and sister to me, and aunts, and company, and food and drink, and (naturally) washing. It's my world, and I don't want any other. What it hasn't got is not worth having, and what it doesn't know is not worth knowing.'

'But isn't it a bit dull at times?' the Mole ventured to ask. 'Just you and the river, and no one else to pass a word with?'

'No one else to – well, I mustn't be hard on you,' said the Rat patiently. 'You're new to it, and of course you don't know. The bank is so crowded nowadays that many people are moving away altogether. O no, it isn't what it used to be, at all. Otters, kingfishers, dabchicks, moorhens, all of them about all day long and always wanting you to do something – as if a fellow had no business of his own to attend to!'

'What lies over *there*?' asked the Mole, waving a paw towards a background of woodland that darkly framed the water-meadows on one side of the river.

'That? O, that's just the Wild Wood,' said the Rat shortly. 'We don't go there very much, we river-bankers.'

'Aren't they – aren't they very nice people in there?' said the Mole a trifle nervously.

'W-e-ll,' replied the Rat, 'let me see. The

laugh. Look here! If you've really nothing else on hand this morning, supposing we drop down the river together, and have a long day of it?'

The Mole waggled his toes from sheer happiness, spread his chest with a sigh of full contentment, and leaned back blissfully into the soft cushions. '*What* a day I'm having!' he said. 'Let us start at once!'

'Hold hard a minute, then!' said the Rat. He looped the painter through a ring in his landing-stage, climbed up into his hole above, and after a short interval reappeared staggering under a fat, wicker luncheon-basket.

'Shove that under your feet,' he said to the Mole, as he passed it down into the boat. Then he untied the painter and took the sculls again.

squirrels are all right. *And* the rabbits – some of 'em, but rabbits are a mixed lot. And then there's Badger, of course. He lives right in the heart of it; wouldn't live anywhere else, either, if you paid him to do it. Dear old Badger! Nobody interferes with him. They'd better not,' he added significantly.

'Why, who *should* interfere with him?' asked the Mole.

'Well, of course – there – are others,' explained the Rat in a hesitating sort of way. 'Weasels – and stoats – and foxes – and so on. They're all right in a way – I'm very good friends with them – pass the time of day when we meet, and all that – but they break out sometimes, there's no denying it, and then – well, you can't really trust them, and that's the fact.'

'And beyond the Wild Wood again?' Mole asked.

'Beyond the Wild Wood comes the Wide World,' said the Rat. 'And that's something that doesn't matter, either to you or me. I've never been there, and I'm never going, nor you either, if you've got any sense at all. Don't ever refer to it again, please. Now then! Here's our backwater at last, where we're going to lunch.'

Leaving the main stream, they now passed into what seemed at first sight like a little landlocked lake. Green turf sloped down to either edge, brown snaky tree-roots gleamed below the surface of the quiet water. It was so very beautiful that the Mole could only hold up both fore-paws and gasp, 'O my! O my! O my!'

The Rat brought the boat alongside the bank, made her fast, helped the Mole safely ashore, and swung out the luncheon-basket. The Mole begged as a favour to be allowed to unpack it all by himself; and the Rat was very pleased to indulge him, and to sprawl at full length on the grass and rest, while his excited friend shook out the table-cloth and spread it, took out all the mysterious packets one by one and arranged their contents in due order, still gasping, 'O my! O my!' at each fresh revelation.

'What are you looking at?' said the Rat presently, when the edge of their hunger was somewhat dulled, and the Mole's eyes were able to wander off the table-cloth a little.

'I am looking,' said the Mole, 'at a streak of bubbles that I see travelling along the surface of the water. That is a thing that strikes me as funny.'

'Bubbles? Oho!' said the Rat, and chirruped cheerily in an inviting sort of way.

A broad glistening muzzle showed itself above the edge of the bank, and the Otter hauled himself out and shook the water from his coat.

'Greedy beggars!' he observed, making for the food. 'Why didn't you invite me, Ratty?'

'This was an unplanned affair,' explained the Rat. 'By the way – my friend, Mr Mole.'

'Proud, I'm sure,' said the Otter, and the two animals were friends forthwith.

There was a rustle behind them, coming from a hedge wherein last year's leaves still clung thick, and a stripy head, with high shoulders behind it, peered forth on them.

'Come on, old Badger!' shouted the Rat.

The Badger trotted forward a pace or two; then grunted, 'H'm! Company,' and turned his back and disappeared from view.

'That's *just* the sort of fellow he is!' observed the disappointed Rat. 'Simply hates Society! Now we shan't see any more of him today. Well, tell us *who's* out on the river?'

'Toad's out, for one,' replied the Otter. 'In his brand-new wager-boat; new togs, new everything!'

The two animals looked at each other and laughed.

'Once, it was nothing but sailing,' said the Rat. 'Then he tired of that and took to punting. Nothing would please him but to punt all day and every day, and a nice mess he made of it. Last year it was house-boating, and we all had to go and stay with him in his house-boat, and pretend we liked it. He was going to spend the rest of his life in a house-boat. It's all the same, whatever he takes up; he gets tired of it, and starts on something fresh.'

'Such a good fellow, too,' remarked the Otter reflectively. 'But no stability – especially in a boat!'

From where they sat they could get a glimpse of the main stream across the island that separated them; and just then a wager-boat flashed into view, the rower – a short,

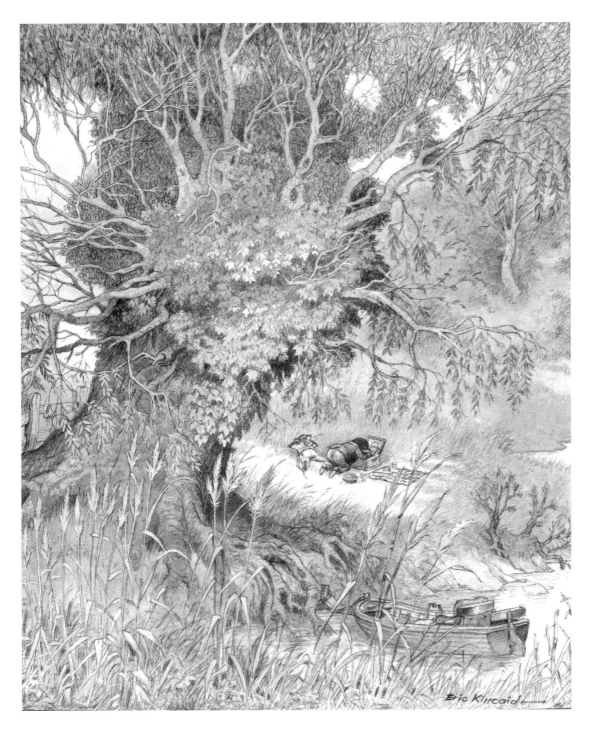

stout figure – splashing badly and rolling a
good deal, but working his hardest. The Rat
stood up and hailed him, but Toad – for it
was he – shook his head and settled sternly
to his work.

'He'll be out of the boat in a minute if he
rolls like that,' said the Rat, sitting down
again.

'Of course he will,' chuckled the Otter.

A mayfly swerved unsteadily across the
current. A swirl of water and a 'cloop!' and
the mayfly was visible no more.

Neither was the Otter.

The Mole looked down. The voice was
still in his ears, but the turf whereon he had
sprawled was clearly vacant. Not an Otter

The Rat shook his head with a smile. 'Not yet, my young friend,' he said – 'wait till you've had a few lessons. It's not as easy as it looks.' But the Mole began to feel more and more jealous of Rat, sculling so strongly and so easily along, and his pride began to whisper that he could do it every bit as well. He jumped up and seized the sculls, so suddenly that the Rat, who was gazing out over the water and saying more poetry-things to himself, was taken by surprise and fell backwards off his seat with his legs in the air for the second time, while the triumphant Mole took his place and grabbed the sculls with entire confidence.

'Stop it, you *silly* fool!' cried the Rat, from the bottom of the boat. 'You can't do it! You'll have us over!'

The Mole flung his sculls back with a flourish, and made a great dig at the water. He missed the surface altogether, his legs flew up above his head, and he found himself lying on the top of the helpless Rat. Greatly alarmed, he made a grab at the side of the boat, and the next moment – Sploosh!

Over went the boat, and he found himself struggling in the river.

O my, how cold the water was, and O, how very wet it felt. How it sang in his ears as he went down, down, down! Then a firm paw gripped him by the back of his neck. It was the Rat, and he was evidently laughing

to be seen, as far as the distant horizon.

But again there was a streak of bubbles on the surface of the river.

'Well, well,' said the Rat, 'I suppose we ought to be moving. I wonder which of us had better pack the luncheon-basket?' he did not speak as if he was frightfully eager for the treat.

'O, please let me,' said the Mole. So, of course, the Rat let him.

The afternoon sun was getting low as the Rat sculled gently homewards in a dreamy mood, murmuring poetry things over to himself, and not paying much attention to Mole. But the Mole was very full of lunch, and self-satisfaction, and already quite at home in a boat (so he thought) and was getting a bit restless besides: and presently he said, 'Ratty! Please, I want to row, now!'

– the Mole could feel him laughing, right down his arm and through his paw, and so into his – the Mole's – neck.

The Rat got hold of a scull and shoved it under the Mole's arm; then he did the same by the other side of him and, swimming behind, propelled the poor animal to shore, hauled him out, and set him down on the bank, a squashy, pulpy lump of misery.

When the Rat had rubbed him down a bit, and wrung some of the wet out of him, he said, 'Now then, old fellow! Trot up and down the towing-path as hard as you can, till you're warm and dry again, while I dive for the luncheon basket.'

So the dismal Mole, wet on the outside and ashamed on the inside, trotted about till he was fairly dry, while the Rat plunged into the water again, recovered the boat, righted her and made her fast, fetched his floating property to shore and finally dived successfully for the luncheon-basket and struggled to land with it.

When all was ready for a start once more, the Mole, limp and dejected, took his seat in the stern of the boat; and as they set off, he said in a low voice, broken with emotion, 'Ratty, my generous friend! I am very sorry indeed for my foolish and ungrateful conduct. My heart quite fails me when I think how I might have lost that beautiful luncheon-basket. Indeed, I have been a complete fool, and I know it. Will you overlook it this once and forgive me, and let things go on as before?'

'That's all right, bless you!' responded the Rat cheerily. 'What's a little wet to a Water Rat! Don't you think any more about it; and look here! I really think you had better come and stop with me for a little time. It's very plain and rough, you know – not like Toad's house at all – but you haven't seen that yet; still, I can make you comfortable.'

The Mole was so touched by the Rat's kind manner of speaking that he could find no voice to answer him; and he had to brush away a tear with the back of his paw. But the Rat kindly looked in another direction, and presently the Mole's spirits revived again, and he was even able to give some straight back-talk to a couple of moorhens who were sniggering to each other about his bedraggled appearance.

When they got home, the Rat made a bright fire in the parlour, and planted the Mole in an armchair in front of it, having fetched down a dressing-gown and slippers for him, and told him river stories till supper-time. Supper was a cheerful meal; but shortly afterwards a sleepy Mole had to be escorted upstairs by his considerate host, to the best bedroom, where he soon laid his head on his pillow in great peace and contentment, knowing that his new-found friend the River was lapping the sill of his window.

This day was only the first of many similar ones for the Mole, each of them longer and fuller of interest as the ripening summer moved onward. He learned to swim and to row, and entered into the joy of running water; and with his ear to the reed-stems he caught, at intervals, something of what the wind was whispering so constantly among them.

CHAPTER 2
THE OPEN ROAD

'Ratty,' said the Mole suddenly, one bright summer morning, 'if you please, I want to ask you a favour. Won't you take me to call on Mr Toad? I've heard so much about him, and I do so want to make his acquaintance.'

'Why, certainly,' said the good-natured Rat, jumping to his feet. 'Get the boat out, and we'll paddle up there at once. It's never the wrong time to call on Toad. Early or late he's always the same fellow. Always good-tempered, always glad to see you, always sorry when you go!'

'He must be a very nice animal,' observed the Mole, as he got into the boat and took the sculls, while the Rat settled himself comfortably in the stern.

'He is indeed the best of animals,' replied Rat. 'So simple, so good-natured, and so affectionate. Perhaps he's not very clever – we can't all be geniuses; and it may be that he is both boastful and conceited. But he has got some great qualities, has Toady.'

Rounding a bend in the river, they came in sight of a handsome, dignified old house of mellowed red brick, with well-kept lawns reaching down to the water's edge.

'There's Toad Hall,' said the Rat. They glided up the creek, and the Mole shipped his sculls as they passed into the shadow of a large boat-house. Here they saw many handsome boats, slung from the cross-beams or hauled up on a slip, but none in the water.

The Rat looked around him. 'I understand,' said he. 'Boating is played out. He's tired of it, and done with it. I wonder what new fad he has taken up now?'

They disembarked, and strolled across the gay flower-decked lawns in search of Toad, whom they soon saw resting in a wicker garden chair, with a preoccupied expression on his face, and a large map spread out on his knees.

'Hooray!' he cried, jumping up on seeing them, 'this is splendid!' He shook the paws of both of them warmly, never waiting for an introduction to the Mole. 'How kind of you!' he went on, dancing round them. 'Come inside and have something! 'You don't know how lucky it is, your turning up just now!'

He led the way to the stable-yard, the Rat following with a most mistrustful expression; and there, drawn out of the coach-house into the open, they saw a gipsy cara-van, shining with newness, painted a canary yellow picked out with green, and red wheels.

'There you are!' cried the Toad, standing before them, legs apart, chest out. 'There's real life for you, embodied in that little cart. The open road, the dusty highway, the heath, the common, the hedgerows, the rolling downs! Camps, villages, towns, cities! Here today, up and off to somewhere else tomorrow! Travel, change, interest, excitement! The whole world before you, and a horizon that's always changing! And mind, this is the very finest cart of its sort that was ever built, without any exception. Come inside and look. Planned it all myself, I did!'

The Mole was tremendously interested and excited, and followed him eagerly up the steps and into the caravan. The Rat only snorted and thrust his hands deep into his pockets, remaining where he was.

It was indeed very compact and comfortable. Little sleeping bunks – a little table that folded up against the wall – a cooking stove, lockers, bookshelves, a bird-cage with a bird in it; and pots, pans, jugs and kettles of every size and variety.

'All complete!' said the Toad triumphantly, pulling open a locker. 'You see – biscuits, potted lobster, sardines – everything – everything you can possibly want. Soda water here – tobacco there – letter paper, bacon, jam, cards and dominoes – you'll find,' he continued, as they descended the steps again, 'you'll find that nothing whatever has been forgotten, when we make our start this afternoon.'

'I beg your pardon,' said the Rat slowly, as he chewed a straw, 'but did I overhear you say something about "*we*", and "*start*", and "*this afternoon*"?'

'Now, you dear good old Ratty,' said Toad imploringly, 'don't begin talking in that stiff and sniffy sort of way, because you know you've got to come. You surely don't mean to stick to your dull smelly old river all your life, and just live in a hole in a bank, and boat? I want to show you the world!'

'I don't care,' said the Rat doggedly. 'I'm not coming, and that's flat. And I *am* going to stick to my old river, *and* live in a hole, *and* boat, as I've always done. And what's more, Mole's going to stick to me and do as I do, aren't you, Mole?'

'Of course I am,' said the Mole loyally. 'I'll always stick to you, Rat, and what you say is to be – has got to be. All the same, it

sounds as if it might have been – well, rather fun, you know!' he added wistfully.

The Rat saw what was passing in his mind, and wavered. He hated disappointing people, and he was fond of the Mole, and would do almost anything to oblige him. Toad was watching both of them closely.

'Come along in and have some lunch,' he said diplomatically, 'and we'll talk it over. We needn't decide anything in a hurry. Of course, I don't really care. I only want to give pleasure to you fellows. "Live for others!" That's my motto in life.'

During lunch – which was excellent, of course, as everything at Toad Hall always was – the Toad simply let himself go. Ignoring the Rat, he painted the prospect of the trip and the joys of the open life and the road-side in such glowing colours that the Mole could hardly sit in his chair for excitement. Somehow, it soon seemed taken for granted by all three of them that the trip was a settled thing; and the Rat, though still unconvinced in his mind, allowed his good nature to over-ride his personal objections. He could not bear to disappoint his two friends, who were already planning out each day's separate occupation for several weeks ahead.

When they were quite ready, the now triumphant Toad led his companions to the paddock and set them to capture the old grey horse, who, without having been consulted, and to his own extreme annoyance, had been chosen by Toad for the dustiest job in this dusty expedition. At last the horse was caught and harnessed, and they set off, all talking at once, each animal either trudging by the side of the cart or sitting on the shaft, as the mood took him. It was a golden afternoon. The smell of the dust they kicked up was rich and satisfying; out of thick orchards on either side of the road, birds called and whistled to them cheerily; good-natured wayfarers, passing them, gave them 'Good day', or stopped to say nice things about their beautiful cart; and rabbits, sitting at their front doors in the hedgerows, held up their fore-paws, and said, 'O my! O my! O my!'

Late in the evening, tired and happy and miles from home, they drew up on a remote common far from any houses, turned the horse loose to graze, and ate their simple supper sitting on the grass by the side of the cart. Then, as night fell, they turned into their little bunks in the cart; and Toad, kicking out his legs, sleepily said, 'Well, good night, you fellows! This is the real life for a gentleman!'

After so much open air and excitement the toad slept very soundly, and no amount of shaking could rouse him out of bed next morning. So the Mole and the Rat set to work, quietly and manfully, and while the Rat saw to the horse, and lit a fire, and cleaned last night's cups and plates, and got things ready for breakfast, the Mole trudged off to the nearest village, a long way off, for milk and eggs and various necessaries the Toad had, of course, forgotten to provide. The hard work had all been done, and the two animals were resting, thoroughly exhausted, by the time Toad appeared on the scene, fresh and gay, remarking what a pleasant easy life it was they were all leading now, after the cares and worries of house-keeping at home.

Their way lay, as before, across country by narrow lanes, and it was not till the afternoon that they came out on the high road, their first high road; and there disaster, sudden and unexpected, sprang out on them – disaster that was momentous indeed to their expedition, but simply overwhelming in its effect on the future career of Toad.

They were strolling along the high road easily, when far behind them they heard a faint warning hum, like the drone of a distant bee. Glancing back, they saw a cloud of dust, with a dark centre, advancing on them

at incredible speed, while from out of the dust a faint 'Poop-poop!' wailed like an uneasy animal in pain. Hardly regarding it, they turned to resume their conversation, when in an instant (as it seemed) the peaceful scene was changed, and with a blast of wind and a whirl of sound that made them jump for the nearest ditch, it was on them! The 'poop-poop' rang with a blaring shout in their ears, they had a moment's glimpse of an interior of glittering plate-glass and rich leather, and the magnificent motor-car, immense, breath-snatching, passionate, with its driver tense and hugging his wheel, claimed all earth and air for a fraction of a second. It flung a cloud of dust that blinded and enwrapped them utterly, and then dwindled to a speck in the far distance, changed back into a droning bee once more.

The old grey horse, dreaming, as he plodded along, of his quiet paddock, in a new situation such as this simply abandoned himself to his natural emotions. Rearing, plunging, backing steadily, in spite of all the Mole's efforts at his head, and all the Mole's lively language appealing to his better nature, he drove the cart backwards towards the deep ditch at the side of the road. It wavered an instant – then there was a heartrending crash – and the canary coloured cart, their pride and their joy, lay on its side in the ditch, a complete wreck.

The Rat danced up and down in the road, simply transported with passion. 'You villains!' he shouted, shaking both fists, 'You scoundrels, you highwaymen, you – you – road-hogs! – I'll have the law on you! I'll report you! I'll take you through all the Courts!'

Toad sat straight down in the middle of the dusty road, his legs stretched out before him, and stared fixedly in the direction of the disappearing motor car. He breathed short, his face wore a placid, satisfied expression, and at intervals he faintly murmured, 'Poop-poop!'

The Mole was busy trying to quiet the horse, which he succeeded in doing after a time. Then he went to look at the cart, on its side in the ditch. It was indeed a sorry sight. Panels and windows smashed, axles hopelessly bent, one wheel off, sardine-tins scattered over the wide world.

The Rat came to help him, but their united efforts were not sufficient to right the cart. 'Hi! Toad!' they cried. 'Come and bear a hand, can't you?'

The Toad never answered a word, or budged from his seat in the road; so they went to see what was the matter with him. They found him in a sort of trance, a happy smile on his face, his eyes still fixed on the dusty wake of their destroyer. At intervals he was still heard to murmur 'Poop-poop!'

The Rat shook him by the shoulder.

'Are you coming to help us, Toad?' he demanded sternly.

'Glorious, stirring sight!' murmured Toad, never offering to move. 'The poetry of motion! The *real* way to travel! The *only* way to travel! Here today – in next week tomorrow! Villages skipped, towns and cities jumped! O bliss! O poop-poop! O my! O my!'

'What are we to do with him?' asked the Mole of the Water Rat.

'Nothing at all,' replied the Rat firmly. 'Because there is really nothing to be done. You see, I know him of old. He is now possessed. He has got a new craze, and it always takes him that way, in its first stage. He'll continue like that for days now, like an animal walking in a happy dream. Never mind him. Let's go and see what there is to be done about the cart.'

A careful inspection showed them that, even if they succeeded in righting it by themselves, the cart would travel no longer. The axles were in a hopeless state, and the missing wheel was shattered into pieces.

The Rat knotted the horse's reins over his back and took him by the head, carrying the bird-cage in the other hand. 'Come on!' he said grimly to the Mole. 'It's five or six miles to the nearest town, and we shall just have to walk it. The sooner we make a start the better.'

'But what about Toad?' asked the Mole anxiously, as they set off together. 'We can't leave him here, sitting in the middle of the road by himself, in the state he's in! It's not safe. Supposing another thing were to come along?'

'O, bother Toad,' said the Rat savagely; 'I've done with him!'

They had not proceeded very far on their way, however, when there was a pattering of feet behind them, and Toad caught them up and thrust a paw inside the elbow of each of them; still breathing short and staring into vacancy.

'Now, look here, Toad!' said the Rat sharply: 'as soon as we get to the town, you'll have to go straight to the police station, and see if they know anything about that motor-car and who it belongs to, and lodge a complaint against it.'

'Police station! Complaint!'murmured Toad dreamily. 'Me *complain* of that beautiful, that heavenly vision! Mend the cart! I've done with carts forever. I never want to see the cart, or to hear of it again.'

The Rat turned from him in despair. 'You see what it is?' he said to the Mole, addressing him across Toad's head: 'He's quite hopeless. I give it up – when we get to the town we'll go to the railway station, and with luck we may pick up a train there that'll get us back to River Bank tonight.'

On reaching the town they went straight to the station and deposited Toad in the second class waiting-room, giving a porter twopence to keep a strict eye on him. They then left the horse at an inn stable, and gave what directions they could about the cart and its contents. Eventually, a slow train having landed them at a station not very far from Toad Hall, they escorted the spellbound, sleepwalking Toad to his door, put him inside it, and instructed his house-keeper to feed him, undress him, and put him to bed. Then they got out their boat from the boat-house, sculled down the river home, and at a very late hour sat down to supper in their own snug little riverside parlour, to the Rat's great joy and contentment.

The following evening the Mole, who had got up late and taken things very easy all day, was sitting on the bank fishing, when the Rat, who had been looking up his friends and gossiping, came strolling along to find him. 'Heard the news?' he said. 'There's nothing else being talked about, all along the river bank. Toad went up to Town by an early train this morning. And he has ordered a very large and very expensive motor-car.'

CHAPTER 3
MR BADGER

The Mole had long wanted to meet the Badger. He seemed, by all accounts, to be such an important person and, though rarely seen, to have an influence on everybody about the place. But whenever the Mole mentioned his wish to the Water Rat he always found himself put off. 'It's all right,' the Rat would say. 'Badger'll turn up some day or other – he's always turning up – and then I'll introduce you. The best of fellows! But you must not only take him as you find him, but *when* you find him.'

'Couldn't you ask him here – dinner or something?' said the Mole.

'He wouldn't come,' replied the Rat simply. 'Badger hates Society, and invitations, and all that sort of thing.'

'Well, then, supposing we go and call on *him*?' suggested the Mole.

'O, I'm sure he wouldn't like that at *all*,' said the Rat, quite alarmed. 'He's so very shy, he'd be sure to be offended. Besides, we can't. It's quite out of the question, because he lives in the very middle of the Wild Wood.'

'Well, supposing he does,' said the Mole. 'You told me the Wild Wood was all right, you know.'

'O, I know, I know, so it is,' replied the Rat. 'But I think we won't go there just now. Not *just* yet.'

The Mole had to be content with this. But the Badger never came along, and it was not till summer was long over, and cold and frost kept them much indoors, and the swollen river raced past outside their windows with a speed that made boating impossible, that he found his thoughts dwelling again on the grey Badger.

In the winter time the Rat slept a great deal, retiring early and rising late.

The Mole had a good deal of spare time on his hands, and so one afternoon, when the Rat in his armchair before the blaze was alternately dozing and trying over rhymes that wouldn't fit, he decided to go out by himself and explore the Wild Wood, and perhaps strike up an acquaintance with Mr Badger.

It was a cold still afternoon with a hard steely sky overhead, when he slipped out of the warm parlour into the open air. The country lay bare and entirely leafless around him as he pushed on towards the Wild Wood, which lay before him low and threatening, like a black reef in some still southern sea.

There was nothing to alarm him at first. Twigs crackled under his feet, logs tripped him, funguses on stumps looked like faces, and startled him for the moment; but that was all fun, and exciting. It led him on, and he went deeper to where the light was less, and trees crouched nearer and nearer, and holes made ugly mouths at him on either side.

Everything was very still now. The dusk advanced on him steadily, rapidly, gathering in behind and in front; and the light seemed to be draining away like floodwater.

Then the faces began. It was over his shoulder that he first thought he saw a face: a little evil wedge-shaped face, looking out at him from a hole. When he turned and confronted it, the thing had vanished.

He quickened his pace, telling himself cheerfully not to begin imagining things, or there would be simply no end to it.

If he could only get away from the holes in the banks, he thought, there would be no more faces. He swung off the path and plunged into the untrodden places of the wood. Then the pattering began.

He thought it was only falling leaves at first, so slight and delicate was the sound of it. Then as it grew it took a regular rhythm, and he knew it for nothing else but the pat-pat-pat of little feet, still a very long way off. Was it in front or behind? It seemed to be first one, then the other, then both. It grew and it multiplied, till from every quarter as he listened anxiously, leaning this way and that, it seemed to be closing in on him.

The pattering increased till it sounded like sudden hail on the dry leaf carpet spread around him. The whole wood seemed running now, running hard, hunting, chasing, closing in round something or – somebody? In panic, he began to run too, aimlessly, he knew not where. He ran up against things, he fell over things and into things, he darted under things and dodged round things. At last he took refuge in the dark deep hollow of an old beech tree, which offered shelter, a hiding place – perhaps even safety, but who could tell?

Meantime the Rat, warm and comfortable, dozed by his fireside. His paper of half-finished verses slipped from his knee, his head fell back, his mouth opened, and he wandered by the grassy banks of dream rivers. Then a coal slipped, the fire crackled and sent up a spurt of flame, and he woke with a start.

He listened for a time. The house seemed very quiet.

Then he called 'Moly!' several times, and, receiving no answer, got up and went out into the hall.

The Mole's cap was missing from its accustomed peg. His galoshes, which always lay by the umbrella stand, were also gone.

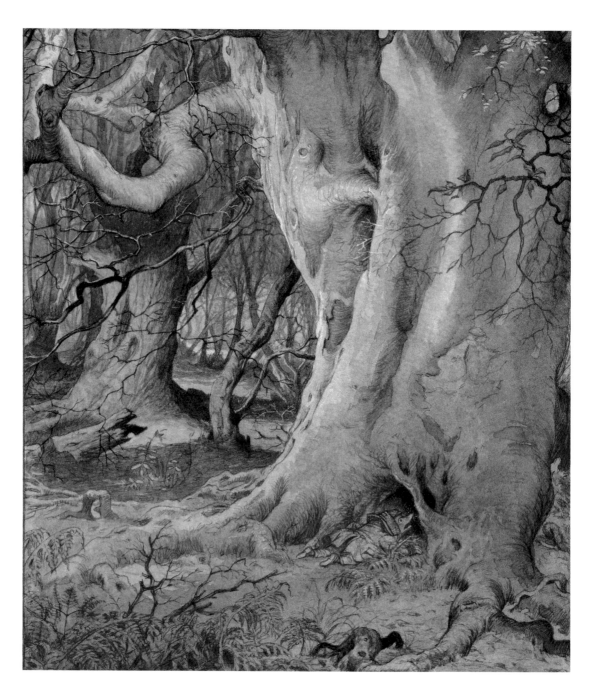

The Rat left the house and carefully examined the muddy surface of the ground outside, hoping to find the Mole's tracks. There they were, sure enough. The galoshes were new, just bought for the winter, and the pimples on their soles were fresh and sharp. He could see the imprints of them in the mud, running along straight and purposeful, leading direct to the Wild Wood.

The Rat looked very grave, and stood in deep thought for a minute or two. Then he re-entered the house, strapped a belt round his waist, shoved a pair of pistols into it, took up a stout cudgel that stood in a corner of the hall, and set off for the Wild Wood at a smart pace.

It was already getting towards dusk when he reached the first fringe of trees and plunged without hesitation into the wood, looking anxiously on either side for any sign of his friend. He made his way manfully through the length of the wood, to its furthest edge, calling out cheerfully, 'Moly, Moly, Moly! Where are you? It's me – it's old Rat!'

He had patiently hunted through the wood for an hour or more, when at last to his joy he heard a little answering cry. Guiding himself by the sound, he made his way through the gathering darkness to the foot of an old beech tree, with a hole in it, and from out of the hole came a feeble voice, saying, 'Ratty! Is that really you?'

The Rat crept into the hollow, and there he found the Mole, exhausted and still trembling. 'O, Rat!' he cried, 'I've been so frightened, you can't think!'

'O, I quite understand,' said the Rat soothingly. 'You shouldn't really have gone and done it, Mole. I did my best to keep you from it. We river-bankers, we hardly ever come here by ourselves. If we have to come, we come in couples, at least; then we're generally all right.'

'Now then,' the Rat continued presently, 'I'll just take a look outside and see if everything's quiet, and then we really must be off.'

He went to the entrance of their retreat and put his head out. Then the Mole heard him saying quietly to himself, 'Hullo! hullo! here – is – a – go!'

'What's up, Ratty?' asked the Mole.

'*Snow* is up,' replied the Rat briefly; 'or rather, *down*. It's snowing hard.'

The Mole came and crouched beside him, and, looking out, saw the wood that had been so dreadful to him in quite a changed aspect. Holes, hollows, pools, pitfalls, and other black menaces to the wayfarer were vanishing fast, and a gleaming carpet of snow was springing up everywhere, that looked too delicate to be trodden upon by rough feet. A fine powder filled the air and caressed the cheek with a tingle in its touch, and the black boles of the

trees showed up in a light that seemed to come from below.

'Well, well, it can't be helped,' said the Rat after pondering. 'We must make a start, and take our chances, I suppose. The worst of it is, I don't exactly know where we are. And now this snow makes everything look so very different.'

It did indeed. The Mole would not have known that it was the same wood. However, they set out bravely, and took the line that seemed most promising, holding on to each other and pretending that they recognised an old friend in every fresh tree that grimly and silently greeted them, or saw openings, gaps, or paths with a familiar turn in them, in the endless scene of white space and black tree trunks that refused to vary.

An hour or two later – they had lost all count of time – they pulled up, downhearted, weary, and hopelessly at sea, and sat down on a fallen tree trunk to recover their breath and consider what was to be done.

'We can't sit here very long,' said the Rat. 'We shall have to make another push for it.'

So once more they got on their feet, and struggled down into the dell, where they hunted about for a cave or some corner that was dry and a protection from the bitter wind and the whirling snow. They were investigating one of the hummocky bits the Rat had spoken of, when suddenly the Mole tripped up and fell forward on his face with a squeal.

'O, my leg!' he cried. 'O, my poor shin!' and he sat up on the snow and nursed his leg in both his front paws.

'Poor old Mole!' said the Rat kindly. 'You don't seem to be having much luck today, do you? Let's have a look at the leg. Yes,' he went on, going down on his knees to look, 'you've cut your shin, sure enough. Wait till I get at my handkerchief, and I'll tie it up for you.'

'I must have tripped over a hidden branch or a stump,' said the Mole miserably. 'O my! O my!'

'It's a very clean cut,' said the Rat, examining it again attentively. 'That was never done by a branch or stump. Looks as if it was made by a sharp edge of something in metal. Funny!' He pondered a while, and examined the humps and slopes that surrounded them.

'Well, never mind what done it,' said the Mole, forgetting his grammar in his pain. 'It hurts just the same, whatever done it.'

But the Rat, after carefully tying up the leg with his handkerchief, had left him and was busy scraping in the snow. He scratched and shovelled and explored, all four legs working busily, while the Mole waited impatiently, remarking at intervals, 'O, come on, Rat!'

Suddenly the Rat cried 'Hooray!' and then 'Hooray-oo-ray-oo-ray-oo-ray!' and danced a feeble jig in the snow.

'What have you found, Ratty?' asked the Mole, still nursing his leg.

'Come and see!' said the delighted Rat, as he jigged on.

The Mole hobbled up to the spot and had a good look.

'Well,' he said at last, slowly, 'I see it right enough. Seen the same sort of thing before, lots of times. Familiar object, I call it. A door-scraper! Well, what of it? Why dance jigs round a door-scraper?'

The Rat didn't reply. He just attacked a snow-bank beside them with great energy, probing with his cudgel everywhere and then digging with fury; and the Mole scraped busily too, more to oblige the Rat than for any other reason, for his opinion was that his friend was getting light-headed.

Some ten minutes' hard work, and the point of the Rat's cudgel struck something that sounded hollow. He worked till he could get a paw through and feel; then called the Mole to come and help him. Hard at it went the two animals, till at last the result of their labours stood in full view of the astonished Mole.

In the side of what had seemed to be a snow-bank stood a solid-looking little door, painted a dark green. An iron bell-pull hung by the side, and below it, on a small brass plate, neatly engraved in square capital letters, they could read by the aid of moonlight: MR BADGER.

The Mole fell backwards on the snow from sheer surprise and delight. 'Rat!' he cried, 'you're a wonder! A real wonder, that's what you are. I see it all now! You're so clever, Ratty–'

'I suppose you're going to sit on the snow all night and talk?' said the Rat crossly. 'Get up at once and hang on to that bell-pull you see there, and ring hard, as hard as you can, while I hammer!'

While the Rat attacked the door with his stick, the Mole sprang up at the bell-pull, clutched it and swung there, both feet well off the ground. From a long way off they could faintly hear a deep-toned bell.

They waited patiently for what seemed a very long time, stamping in the snow to keep their feet warm. At last they heard the sound of slow shuffling footsteps approaching the door from the inside.

There was the noise of a bolt shot back, and the door opened a few inches, enough to show a long snout and a pair of sleepy blinking eyes.

'Now, the *very* next time this happens,' said a gruff voice, 'I shall be exceedingly angry. Who is it *this* time, disturbing people on such a night? Speak up!'

'O, Badger,' cried the Rat, 'let us in, please. It's me, Rat, and my friend Mole, and we've lost our way in the snow.'

'What, Ratty, my dear little man!' exclaimed the Badger, in quite a different voice. 'Come along in, both of you, at once. Why, you must be frozen. Well I never! Lost in the snow! And in the Wild Wood too, and at this time of night! But come in.'

The two animals tumbled over each other in their eagerness to get inside, and with great joy and relief heard the door shut behind them.

The Badger shuffled on in front of them, carrying a candle, and they followed him, nudging each other in an excited sort of way, down a long, gloomy, and to tell the truth, decidedly shabby passage, into a sort of a central hall, out of which they could dimly see other long tunnel-like passages. But there were doors in the hall as well – stout oak doors. One of these the Badger flung open, and at once they found themselves in all the glow and warmth of a large fire-lit kitchen.

The kindly Badger sat them down on seats to toast themselves at the fire, and made them remove their wet coats and boots. Then he fetched them dressing-gowns and slippers, and bathed the Mole's shin with warm water and mended the cut with sticking plaster till the whole thing was just as good as new, if not better. In the embracing light and warmth, warm and dry at last, with weary legs propped up in front of them, and the cheering clink of plates

being arranged on the table behind, it seemed to the storm-driven animals that the cold and trackless Wild Wood just left out-side was miles and miles away, and all that they had suffered in it a half-forgotten dream.

When at last they were thoroughly toasted, the Badger summoned them to the table, where he had been busy laying a meal. They had felt pretty hungry before, but when they actually saw at last the sup-per that was spread for them, really it seemed only a question of what they should attack first where all was so attractive, and whether the other things would obligingly wait for them till they had time to give them attention.

When supper was really finished at last, and after they had chatted for a time about things in general, the Badger said heartily, 'Now then! Tell us the news from your part of the world. How's old Toad going on?'

'O, from bad to worse,' said the Rat, while the Mole, basking in the firelight, his heels higher than his head, tried to look properly mournful. 'Another smash-up only last week, and a bad one. You see, he *will* insist on driving himself, and he's hopeless-ly incapable. If he'd only employ a decent, steady, well-trained animal, pay him good wages, and leave everything to him, he'd get on all right. But no; he thinks he's a heaven-born driver, and nobody can teach him anything; and all the rest follows.'

'How many has he had?' asked the Badger gloomily.

'Smashes, or machines?' asked the Rat. 'O, well, after all, it's the same thing – with Toad. This is the seventh. As for the others – you know that coach-house of his? Well, it's piled up – piled up to the roof – with bits of motor cars, none of them bigger than your hat! That accounts for the other six – so far as they can be accounted for.'

'He's been in hospital three times,' put in the Mole; 'and as for the fines he's had to pay, it's simply awful to think of.'

'Yes, and that's part of the trouble,' continued the Rat. 'Toad's rich, we all know; but he's not a millionaire. And he's a hopelessly bad driver, and quite regardless of law and order. Killed or ruined – it's got to be one of the two things, sooner or later. Badger! We're his friends – oughtn't we to do something?'

The Badger went through a bit of hard thinking. 'Now look here!' he said at last, rather severely; 'of course you know I can't do anything *now*?'

His two friends agreed, quite understanding his point. No animal is ever expected to do anything strenuous, or heroic, or even moderately active during the off-season of winter.

'Very well then!' continued the Badger. '*But*, when once the year has really turned, and the nights are shorter, and halfway through them one rouses and feels fidgety and wanting to be up and doing by sunrise, if not before – you know!'

Both animals nodded gravely. *They* knew!

'Well, *then*,' went on the Badger, 'we – that is, you and me and our friend the Mole here – we'll take Toad in hand. We'll stand no nonsense whatever. We'll bring him back to reason, by force if need be. We'll *make* him be a sensible Toad. We'll – you're asleep, Rat!'

'Not me!' said the Rat, waking up with a jump.

'Well, it's time we were all in bed,' said the Badger, getting up and fetching flat candlesticks. 'Come along, you two, and I'll show you your quarters. And take your time tomorrow morning – breakfast at any hour you please!'

* * *

During lunch the next day, the Badger and the Mole became very friendly, after the Mole had expressed his preference for underground homes. As soon as lunch was

over the Badger offered to show the Mole around his house.

The Badger lighted a lantern and told the Mole to follow him. Crossing the hall, they passed down one of the principal tunnels, and the wavering light of the lantern gave glimpses on either side of rooms both large and small, some mere cupboards, others nearly as broad and imposing as Toad's dining hall. A narrow passage at right-angles led them into another corridor, and here the same thing was repeated. The Mole was staggered at the size and extent of it all; at the length of the dim passages, the solid ceilings of the crammed store chambers, the stonework everywhere, the pillars, the arches, the pavements. 'How on earth, Badger,' the Mole said at last, 'did you ever find time and strength to do all this? It's astonishing!'

'It *would* be astonishing indeed,' said the Badger simply, 'if I had done it. But as a matter of fact I did none of it – only cleaned out the passages and rooms, as far as I had need of them. There's lots more of it, all round about. I see you don't understand, and I must explain it to you. Well, very long ago, on the spot where the Wild Wood now thrust into his belt again. 'Come along, Mole,' he said, as soon as he caught sight of them. 'We must get off while it's daylight. Don't want to spend another night in the Wild Wood again.'

'You really needn't fret, Ratty,' added the Badger placidly. 'My passages run further than you think, and I've bolt-holes to the edge of the wood in several directions, though I don't care for everybody to know them. When you really have to go, you shall leave by one of my shortcuts. Meantime, make yourself easy, and sit down again.'

The Rat was nevertheless still eager to be off and attend to his river, so the Badger, taking up his lantern again, led the way along a damp and airless tunnel that wound and dipped for a weary distance that seemed to be miles. At last daylight began to show itself through tangled growth over-hanging the mouth of the passage; and the Badger, bidding them a hasty good-bye, pushed them through the opening, made everything look as natural as possible again, with creepers, brushwood, and dead leaves, and retreated.

They found themselves standing on the very edge of the Wild Wood. Rocks and brambles and tree-roots behind them; in front a great space of quiet fields, hemmed by lines of hedges black on the snow, and, far ahead, a glint of the familiar old river, while the wintry sun hung red and low on the horizon. Looking back, they saw the whole mass of the Wild Wood, dense, men-acing, compact, grimly set in vast white sur-rounding; together they turned and made swiftly for home, for firelight, and for the voice, sounding cheerily outside their win-dow, of the river that they knew and trust-ed in all its moods.

stands, before ever it had planted itself and grown up to what it now is, there was a city – a city of people, you know.

'But what has become of them all?' asked the Mole.

'Who can tell?' said the Badger. 'People come – they stay for a while, they build – and they go. It is their way. But we remain. There were badgers here. I've been told, long before that same city ever came to be. And now there are badgers here again.'

When they got back to the kitchen again, they found the Rat walking up and down, very restless. The underground atmosphere was getting on his nerves, and he seemed really to be afraid that the river would run away if he wasn't there to look after it. So he had his overcoat on, and his pistols

CHAPTER 4
MR TOAD

It was a bright morning in the early part of summer; the river had sunk back to its normal banks and its usual pace, and a hot sun seemed to be pulling everything green and bushy and spiky up out of the earth towards him, as if by strings. The Mole and the Water Rat had been up since dawn, very busy on matters connected with boats and the opening of the boating season; painting and varnishing, mending paddles, repairing cushions, hunting for missing boat hooks, and so on; and were finishing breakfast in their little parlour and eagerly discussing their plans for the day, when a heavy knock sounded at the door.

The Mole went to answer the door, and the Rat heard him utter a cry of surprise. Then he flung the parlour door open, and announced with much importance, 'Mr Badger!'

This was a wonderful thing, indeed, that the Badger should pay a call on them, or indeed on anybody.

The Badger strode heavily into the room, and stood looking at the two animals with an expression full of seriousness. The Rat let his egg-spoon fall on the table cloth, and sat open-mouthed.

'The hour has come!' said the Badger at last.

'*What* hour?' asked the Rat uneasily, glancing at the clock on the mantelpiece.

'Whose hour, you should rather say,' replied the Badger. 'Why, Toad's hour! The hour of Toad! I said I would take him in hand as soon as the winter was well over, and I'm going to take him in hand today!'

'Toad's hour, of course!' cried the Mole delightedly. 'Hooray! I remember now! *We'll* teach him to be a sensible Toad!'

'This very morning,' continued the Badger, taking an armchair, 'as I learned last night from a trustworthy source, another new and very powerful motor-car will arrive at Toad Hall on approval or return.'

'Right you are!' cried the Rat, starting up. 'We'll rescue the poor unhappy animal! We'll change him! He'll be the most changed Toad that ever was before we've done with him!'

They set off up the road, Badger leading the way. They reached the carriage drive of Toad Hall to find, as the Badger had expected, a shiny new motor-car, of great size, painted a bright red, standing in front of the house. As they neared the door it was flung open, and Mr Toad, dressed in goggles, cap, gaiters, and enormous overcoat, came swaggering down the steps, drawing on his gloves.

'Hullo! come on, you fellows!' he cried cheerfully on catching sight of them. 'You're just in time to come with me for a – to come for a – for a – er–'

His hearty voice fell away as he noticed the stern unbending look on the faces of his silent friends, and his invitation remained unfinished.

The Badger strode up the steps. 'Take him inside,' he said sternly to his companions. Then, as Toad was hustled through the door, struggling and protesting, he turned to the chauffeur in charge of the new motor-car.

'I'm afraid you won't be wanted today,' he said. 'Mr Toad has changed his mind. He will not require the car. Please understand that this is final. You needn't wait.' Then he followed the others inside and shut the door.

'Now, then!' he said to the Toad, when the four of them stood together in the hall, 'first of all, take those ridiculous things off!'

'Shan't!' replied Toad, with great spirit. 'What is the meaning of this outrage! I demand an instant explanation.'

'Take them off him, then, you two,' ordered the Badger briefly.

They had to lay Toad out on the floor, kicking and calling all sorts of names, before they could get to work properly. Then the Rat sat on him, and the Mole got his motor clothes off him bit by bit, and they stood him up on his legs again.

'You knew it must come to this, sooner or later, Toad,' the Badger explained severely. 'You've disregarded all the warnings we've given you, you've gone on wasting the money your father left you, and you're getting us animals a bad name in the district by your furious driving and your smashes and your rows with the police. You will come with me into the smoking room, and there you will hear some facts about yourself; and we'll see whether you come out of that room the same Toad that you went in.'

He took Toad firmly by the arm, led him into the smoking room, and closed the door behind them.

'*That's* no good!' said the Rat. '*Talking* to Toad'll never cure him. He'll say anything.'

They made themselves comfortable in armchairs and waited patiently. Through the closed door they could just hear the long drone of the Badger's voice, rising and falling in waves; and presently they heard long-drawn sobs, seeming to come from Toad, who was a soft-hearted and affectionate fellow, very easily converted – for the time being – to any point of view.

After some three-quarters of an hour the door opened, and the Badger reappeared, leading by the paw a very limp and dejected Toad. His skin hung baggily about him, his legs wobbled, and his cheeks were lined with tears.

'Sit down there, Toad,' said the Badger kindly, pointing to a chair. 'My friends,' he went on, 'I am pleased to inform you that Toad has at last seen the error of his ways. He is truly sorry for his misguided conduct in the past, and he has agreed to give up motor cars entirely and forever. I have his solemn promise to that effect.'

'That is very good news,' said the Mole gravely.

'Very good news indeed,' said the Rat doubtfully, '*if* only – if only – '

He was looking very hard at Toad as he said this, and could not help thinking he was something like a twinkle in that animal's still sorrowful eyes.

'There's only one thing more to be done,' continued the Badger.

'Repeat, before your friends here, what you fully admitted to me in the smoking room just now. First, you are sorry for what you've done, and you see the folly of it all.'

There was a long, long pause. Toad looked this way and that, while the other animals waited in silence. At last he spoke.

'No!' he said a little sulkily, but stoutly, 'I'm not sorry. And it wasn't folly at all! It was simply glorious!'

'What?' cried the Badger, greatly shocked. 'You backsliding animal, didn't you tell me just now, in there–'

'O, yes, yes, in *there*,' said Toad impatiently. 'I'd have said anything in there. You're so eloquent, dear Badger, and so moving, and so convincing, and put all your points so very well – you can do what you like with me in there, and you know it. But I've been searching my mind since, and going over things in it, and I find that I'm not a bit sorry really, so it's no earthly good

saying I am; now, is it?'

'Then you don't promise,' said the Badger, 'never to touch a motor-car again?'

'Certainly not!' replied Toad. 'On the contrary, I faithfully promise that the very first motor-car I see, poop-poop! off I go in it!'

'Told you so, didn't I?' said the Rat to the Mole.

'Very well, then,' said the Badger firmly, rising to his feet. 'Since you won't be reasonable, we'll try what force can do. I feared it would come to this all along. You've often asked us three to come and stay with you, Toad, in this handsome house of yours; well, now we're going to. When we've converted you to a proper point of view we may quit, but not before. Take him upstairs, you two, and lock him up in his bedroom, while we arrange matters between ourselves.'

'It's for your own good, Toady, you know,' said the Rat kindly, as Toad, kicking and struggling, was hauled up the stairs by his two faithful friends.

'Think what fun we shall all have together, just as we used to, when you've quite got over this – this painful attack of yours!'

'We'll take great care of everything for you till you're well, Toad,' said the Mole; 'and we'll see your money isn't wasted, as it has been.'

'No more of those regrettable incidents with the police, Toad,' said the Rat, as they thrust him into his bedroom.

'And no more weeks in hospital, being ordered about by female nurses, Toad,' added the Mole, turning the key on him.

They went downstairs, Toad shouting abuse at them through the keyhole; and the three friends then met in conference on the situation.

'It's going to be a tiresome business,' said the Badger, sighing. 'I've never seen Toad so determined. However, we will see it out. He must never be left an instant unguarded. We shall have to take it in turns to be with him, till the poison has worked itself out of his system.'

They arranged to keep watch over him. Each animal took it in turns to sleep in Toad's room at night, and they divided the day up between them.

One fine morning the Rat, whose turn it was to go on duty, went upstairs to relieve Badger, whom he found fidgeting to be off and stretch his legs in a long ramble round his wood and down his earths and burrows. 'Toad's still in bed,' he told the Rat, outside the door.

'Can't get much out of him, except, "O, leave him alone, he wants nothing, perhaps he'll be better presently, it may pass off in time, don't be unduly anxious," and so on. Now, you look out, Rat! When Toad's quiet and obedient, then he's at his most artful. There's sure to be something up. I know him. Well, now I must be off.'

'How are you today, old chap?' asked the Rat cheerfully, as he approached Toad's bedside.

He had to wait some minutes for an answer. At last a feeble voice replied, 'Thank you so much, dear Ratty! But first tell me how you are yourself, and the excellent Mole?'

'O, *we're* all right,' replied the Rat. 'Mole,' he added carelessly, 'is going out for a run-round with Badger. They'll be out till lunchtime, so you and I will spend a pleasant morning together, and I'll do my best to amuse you. Now jump up, there's a good fellow, and don't lie moping there on a fine morning like this!'

'Dear, kind Rat,' murmured Toad, 'how little you realise my condition, and how very far I am from "jumping up" now – if ever! But do not trouble about me. I hate being a burden to my friends, and I do not expect to be one much longer. Indeed, I almost hope not.'

'You are, indeed a burden,' said the Rat. 'But I tell you, I'd take any trouble on earth for you, if only you'd be a sensible animal.'

'If I thought that, Ratty,' murmured Toad, more feebly than ever, 'then I would beg you – for the last time, probably – to step round to the village as quickly as possible – even now it may be too late – and fetch the doctor. But don't you bother. It's only a trouble, and perhaps we may as well let things take their course.'

'Why, what do you want a doctor for?' asked the Rat, coming closer and examining him. He certainly lay very still and flat, and his voice was weaker and his manner much changed.

'Surely you have noticed of late,' murmured Toad. 'But no – why should you? Noticing things is only a trouble. Tomorrow, indeed, you may be saying to yourself, "O, if only I had noticed sooner! If only I had done something!" But no; it's a trouble. Never mind – forget that I asked.'

'Look here, old man,' said the Rat, beginning to get rather alarmed, 'of course I'll fetch a doctor to you, if you really think you want him. But you can hardly be bad enough for that yet. Let's talk about something else.'

'I fear, dear friend,' said Toad, with a sad smile, 'that "talk" can do little in a case like this – or doctors either, for that matter; still one must grasp at the slightest straw. And, by the way – while you are about it – I hate

to give you more trouble, but I happen to remember that you will pass the door – would you mind at the same time asking the lawyer to step up? It would be a convenience to me, and there are moments – perhaps I should say there is a moment – when one must face disagreeable tasks, at whatever cost to exhausted nature!'

'A lawyer! O, he must be really bad!' the worried Rat said to himself, as he hurried from the room, not forgetting, however, to lock the door carefully behind him.

Outside, he stopped to consider. The other two were far away, and he had no one to consult.

'It's best to be on the safe side,' he said.

So he ran off to the village on his errand of mercy.

The Toad, who had hopped lightly out of bed as soon as he heard the key turned in the lock, watched him eagerly from the window till he disappeared down the drive. Then, laughing heartily, he dressed as quickly as possible in the smartest suit he could lay hands on at the moment, filled his pockets with cash which he took from a small drawer in the dressing-table, and next, knotting the sheets from his bed together and tying one end round the central bar of the window, he scrambled out, slid lightly to the ground, and, taking the opposite direction to the Rat, marched off lightheartedly, whistling a merry tune.

It was a gloomy lunch for Rat when the Badger and the Mole at length returned, and he had to face them at table with his rather weak story. The Badger's biting, not

to say brutal, remarks may be imagined; but it was painful to the Rat that even the Mole, though he took his friend's side as far as possible, could not help saying, 'You've been a bit of a duffer this time, Ratty! Toad, too, of all animals!'

'He did it awfully well,' said the Rat.

'He did *you* awfully well!' replied the Badger hotly. 'However, talking won't mend matters. He's got clear away for the time, that's certain; and the worst of it is, he'll be so conceited with what he'll think is his cleverness that he may do anything. One comfort is, we're free now, and needn't waste any more of our precious time doing sentry duty. But we'd better continue to sleep at Toad Hall for a while longer. Toad may be brought at any moment – on a stretcher, or between two policemen.'

So spoke the Badger, not knowing what the future held in store, or how much water was to run under bridges before toad should sit at ease again in his ancestral Hall.

* * *

Meanwhile, Toad was walking briskly along the high road, some miles from home. At first he had taken bypaths, and crossed many fields, and changed his course several times, in case of pursuit; but now, feeling by this time safe from recapture, and the sun smiling brightly on him, he almost danced along the road.

'Smart piece of work that!' he remarked to himself, chuckling. 'Brain against brute force – and brain came out on the top – as it's bound to do. Poor old Ratty! My! won't he catch it when the Badger gets back! A worthy fellow, Ratty, with many good qualities, but very little intelligence and absolutely no education. I must take him in hand some day, and see if I can make something of him.'

Filled full of conceited thoughts such as these he strode along, his head in the air, till he reached a little town, where the sign of

'The Red Lion', swinging across the road halfway down the main street, reminded him that he had not had breakfast that day, and that he was very hungry after his long walk. He marched into the inn, ordered the best lunch that could be provided at so short a notice, and sat down to eat it in the coffee room.

He was about halfway through his meal when an only too familiar sound, approaching down the street, made him start and fall trembling all over. The poop-poop! drew nearer and nearer, the car could be heard to turn into the inn yard and come to a stop, and Toad had to hold on to the leg of the table to hide his feelings. Presently the party entered the coffee room, hungry and talkative. Toad listened eagerly, all ears, for a time; at last he could stand it no longer. He slipped out of the room quietly, paid his bill at the bar, and as soon as he got outside sauntered round quietly to the inn yard. 'There cannot be any harm,' he said to himself, 'in my only just *looking* at it!'

The car stood in the middle of the yard, quite unattended, the stable helps being all at their dinner. Toad walked slowly round it, inspecting, criticising, thinking deeply.

'I wonder,' he said to himself presently, 'I wonder if this sort of car *starts* easily?'

Next moment, hardly knowing how it came about, he found he had hold of the handle and was turning it. As the familiar sound broke forth, the old passion came back and completely mastered Toad, body and soul. As if in a dream he found himself, somehow, seated in the driver's seat; as if in a dream, he pulled the lever and swung the car round the yard and out through the archway; and, as if in a dream, all sense of right and wrong seemed temporarily suspended. He increased his pace, and as the car leapt forth on the high road through the open country, he only knew that he was Toad once more, Toad at his best and highest, Toad the terror, the Lord of the lone

trail, before whom all must give way. The miles were eaten up under him as he sped he knew not where, living his hour, not caring what might happen to him.

* * *

'To my mind,' observed the Chairman of the Bench of Magistrates cheerfully, 'the *only* difficulty that presents itself in this otherwise very clear case is, how we can possibly make it sufficiently hot for the incorrigible rogue and hardened ruffian whom we see cowering in the dock before us. Let me see: he has been found guilty, on the clearest evidence, first, of stealing a valuable motor-car; secondly, of driving to the public danger; and, thirdly, of gross impertinence to the police. Mr Clerk, will you tell us, please, what is the very stiffest penalty we can impose for each of these offences? Without, of course, giving the prisoner the benefit of any doubt, because there isn't any.'

The Clerk scratched his nose with his pen. 'Some people would consider,' he observed, 'that stealing the motor-car was upon the hapless Toad, loaded him with chains, and dragged him from the Court House, shrieking, praying, protesting; across the market place, where the playful crowd assailed him with jeers, carrots, and popular catch-words; past hooting school children, their innocent faces lit up with the pleasure they derive from the sight of a gentleman in difficulties; across the hollow-sounding drawbridge, below the spiky portcullis, under the frowning archway of the grim old castle, whose ancient towers soared high overhead; past the turning that led to the private scaffold, till they reached the door of the grimmest dungeon that lay in the heart of the innermost keep. There at last they paused, where an ancient gaoler sat fingering a bunch of mighty keys.

The gaoler grimly laid his withered hand on the shoulder of the miserable Toad. The rusty key creaked in the lock, the great door clanged behind them; and Toad was a help-less prisoner in the remotest dungeon of the best-guarded keep of the stoutest castle in all the length and breadth of Merry England.

the worst offence; and so it is. But cheeking the police undoubtedly carries the severest penalty; and so it ought. Supposing you were to say twelve months for the theft, which is mild; and three years for the furi-ous driving, which is lenient; and fifteen years for the cheek, which was pretty bad sort of cheek, judging by what we've heard from the witness box, even if you only believe one tenth part of what you heard, and I never believe more myself – those fig-ures, if added together correctly, tot up to nineteen years–'

'First rate!' said the Chairman.

'–So you had better make it a round twenty years and be on the safe side,' ended the Clerk.

'An excellent suggestion!' said the Chairman approvingly. 'Prisoner! Pull your-self together and try and stand up straight. It's going to be twenty years for you this time. And mind, if you appear before us again, upon any charge whatsoever, we shall have to deal with you very seriously!'

Then the brutal minions of the law fell

CHAPTER 5

TOAD'S ADVENTURES

When Toad found himself locked away in a damp and evil-smelling dungeon, and knew that all the grim darkness of a medieval fortress lay between him and the outer world of sunshine and high roads where he had lately been so happy, he flung himself at full length on the floor, and shed bitter tears, and abandoned himself to dark despair. 'Stupid animal that I was' (he said), 'now I must languish in this dungeon, till people who were proud to say they knew me, have forgotten the very name of Toad! O wise old Badger!' (he said), 'O clever, intelligent Rat and sensible Mole! What sound judgements, what a knowledge of men and matters you possess! O unhappy and forsaken Toad!' With lamentations such as these he passed his days and nights for several weeks, refusing his meals or light refreshments, though the grim and ancient gaoler, knowing that Toad's pockets were well lined, frequently pointed out that many comforts, and indeed luxuries, could by arrangement be sent in – at a price – from outside.

Now the gaoler had a pleasant and good-hearted daughter, who assisted her father in the lighter duties of his post. She was particularly fond of animals, and, besides her canary, she kept several piebald mice and a restless squirrel.

This kind-hearted girl, pitying the misery of Toad, said to her father one day, 'Father! I can't bear to see that poor beast so unhappy, and getting so thin! You let me have the managing of him. You know how fond of animals I am. I'll make him eat from my hand, and sit up, and do all sorts of things.'

Her father replied that she could do what she liked with him. He was tired of Toad, and his sulks and his airs and his meanness. So that day she went on her errand of mercy, and knocked at the door of Toad's cell.

'Now, cheer up, Toad,' she said coaxingly, on entering, 'and sit up and dry your eyes and be a sensible animal. And do try and eat a bit of dinner. See, I've brought you some of mine, hot from the oven!'

It was bubble and squeak, between two plates, and its fragrance filled the narrow cell. The penetrating smell of cabbage reached the nose of Toad as he lay in his misery on the floor. It gave him the idea for a moment that perhaps life was not such a bleak and desperate thing as he had imagined. But still he wailed, and kicked with his legs, and refused to be comforted. So the wise girl retired for the time, but, of course, a good deal of the smell of hot cabbage remained behind, as it will do, and Toad, between his sobs, sniffed and reflected, and gradually began to think new and inspiring thoughts: of chivalry, and poetry, and deeds still to be done; of broad meadows, and cattle browsing in them, raked by sun and wind; of kitchen gardens, and straight herb-borders, and warm snapdragons beset by bees; and of the comforting clink of dishes set down on the table at Toad Hall, and the scrape of chair legs on the floor as everyone pulled himself close up to his work. The air of the narrow cell took on a rosy tinge; he began to think of his friends, and how they would surely be able to do something; of lawyers, and how they would have enjoyed his case, and what a fool he had been not to get in a few; and lastly, he thought of his own great cleverness, and all that he was capable of if he only gave his great mind to it; and the cure was almost complete.

When the girl returned, some hours later, she carried a tray, with a cup of fragrant tea steaming on it; and a plate piled up with very hot buttered toast, cut thick, very brown on both sides, with the butter running through the holes in it in great golden drops, like honey from the honeycomb. The smell of that buttered toast simply talked to Toad, and with no uncertain voice; talked of warm kitchens, of breakfasts on bright frosty mornings, and of snug parlour firesides on winter evenings. Toad sat up on end once more, dried his eyes, sipped his tea and munched his toast, and soon began talking freely about himself, and the house he lived in, and his doings there, and how important he was, and how much his friends thought of him.

The gaoler's daughter saw that the topic was doing him as much good as the tea, as indeed it was, and encouraged him to go on.

They had many interesting talks together, after that, as the dreary days went on; and the gaoler's daughter grew very sorry for Toad, and thought it a great shame that a poor little animal should be locked up in prison for what seemed to her a very unimportant crime. Toad, of course, in his vanity, thought that her interest in him came from a growing tenderness; and he could not help half regretting that the social gulf between them was so very wide, for she was a pretty lass, and evidently admired him very much.

One morning the girl was very thoughtful and did not seem to Toad to be paying proper attention to his witty sayings and sparkling comments.

'Toad,' she said presently, 'just listen, please. I have an aunt who is a washer-

woman.'

'There, there,' said Toad, 'never mind; think no more about it. *I* have several aunts who *ought* to be washerwomen.'

'Do be quiet a minute, Toad,' said the girl. 'You talk too much, that's your chief fault, and I'm trying to think, and you hurt my head. As I said, I have an aunt who is a washerwoman; she does the washing for all the prisoners in this castle – we try to keep any paying business of that sort in the family, you understand. She takes out the washing on Monday morning, and brings it in on Friday evening. This is a Thursday. Now, this is what occurs to me: you're very rich – at least you're always telling me so – and she's very poor. A few pounds wouldn't make any difference to you, and it would mean a lot to her. Now, I think if she were properly approached – squared, I believe, is the word you animals use – you could come to some arrangement by which she would let you have her dress and bonnet and so on, and you could escape from the castle as the official washerwoman. You're very alike in many respects – particularly about the figure.'

'We're *not*,' said the Toad in a huff. 'I have a very elegant figure – for what I am.'

'So has my aunt,' replied the girl, 'for what *she* is. But have it your own way. You horrid, proud, ungrateful animal, when I'm sorry for you, and trying to help you!'

'Yes, yes, that's all right; thank you very much indeed,' said the Toad hurriedly. 'But look here! You wouldn't surely have Mr Toad, of Toad Hall, going about the country disguised as a washerwoman!'

'Then you can stop here as a Toad,' replied the girl with much spirit. 'I suppose you want to go off in a horse-driven coach!'

Honest Toad was always ready to admit himself in the wrong. 'You are a good, kind, clever girl,' he said, 'and I am indeed a proud and a stupid toad. Introduce me to your worthy aunt, if you will be so kind, and I have no doubt that the excellent lady and I will be able to arrange terms satisfactory to both parties.'

Next evening the girl took her aunt into Toad's cell, bearing his week's washing pinned up in a towel. The old lady had been prepared beforehand for the interview, and the sight of certain golden coins that Toad had thoughtfully placed on the table in full view practically completed the matter and left little further to discuss. In return for his cash, Toad received a cotton print gown, an apron, a shawl, and a black bonnet; the only demand the old lady made was that she should be gagged and bound and dumped down in a corner. By this trick, she explained, no one would think she had helped Toad escape.

Toad was delighted with the suggestion. It would enable him to leave the prison in some style, and with his reputation for being a desperate and dangerous fellow unharmed; and he readily helped the gaoler's daughter to make her aunt appear as much as possible the victim of circumstances over which she had no control.

'Now it's your turn, Toad,' said the girl. 'Take off that coat and waistcoat of yours; you're fat enough as it is.'

Shaking with laughter, she proceeded to dress him in the cotton print gown, arranged the shawl around him, and tied the strings of the bonnet under his chin.

'You're the very image of her,' she giggled, 'only I'm sure you never looked half so respectable in all your life before. Now, goodbye, Toad, and good luck. Go straight down the way you came up; and if anyone says anything to you, as they probably will, being but men, you can answer back a bit, of course, but remember you're a widow woman, quite alone in the world.'

With a quaking heart, but as firm a footstep as he could command, Toad set forth; but he was soon agreeably surprised to find how easy everything was made for him. The washerwoman's dumpy figure in its familiar cotton print seemed a passport for every barred door and grim gateway; even when he hesitated, uncertain as to the right turning to take, he found himself helped out of his difficulty by the warder at the next gate, anxious to be off to his tea.

It seemed hours before he crossed the last courtyard, rejected the pressing invitations from the last guardroom, and dodged the outspread arms of the last warder, pleading for just one farewell embrace. But at last he heard the wicket-gate in the great outer door click behind him, felt the fresh air of the outer world upon his brow, and knew that he was free!

Dizzy with the easy success of his daring exploit, he walked quickly towards the lights of the town, not knowing in the least what he should do next, only quite certain of one thing, that he must remove himself as quickly as possible from the neighbourhood.

As he walked along, considering, his attention was caught by some red and green lights a little way off, to one side of the town, and the sound of the puffing and snorting of engines and the banging of shunted trucks fell on his ear. 'Aha!' he thought, 'this is a piece of luck! A railway station is the thing I want most in the whole world at this moment.'

He made his way to the station, looked at a timetable, and found that a train, bound more or less in the direction of his home, was due to start in half an hour. 'More luck!' said Toad, his spirits rising rapidly, and went off to the booking office to buy his ticket. He gave the name of the station that he knew to be nearest to Toad Hall and put his fingers, in search of the necessary money, where his waistcoat pocket should have been.

To his horror he remembered that he had left both coat and waistcoat behind him in his cell, and with them his pocket-book, money, keys, watch, matches, pencil case – all that makes life worth living, all that sets the many pocketed animal above the inferior one-pocketed or no-pocketed types.

In his misery he made one desperate effort to carry the thing off, and, with a return to his fine old manner, he said, 'Look here! I find I've left my purse behind. Just give me that ticket, will you, and I'll send the money on tomorrow. I'm well known in these parts.'

The clerk stared at him and the black bonnet a moment, and then laughed. 'I should think you were pretty well known in these parts,' he said, 'if you've tried this game on often. Here, stand away from the window, please, madam; you're blocking the other passengers!'

Baffled and full of despair, he wandered blindly down the platform where the train was standing, and tears trickled down each side of his nose.

'Hullo, mother!' said the engine-driver, 'what's the trouble? You don't look particularly cheerful.'

'O, sir!' said Toad, crying afresh, 'I am a poor unhappy washerwoman, and I've lost all my money, and can't pay for a ticket, and I *must* get home tonight somehow, and whatever I am to do I don't know. O dear, O dear!'

'That's a bad business, indeed,' said the engine driver. 'Lost your money – and can't get home – and got some kids, too, waiting for you, I dare say?'

'Any amount of 'em,' sobbed Toad. 'And they'll be hungry – and playing with matches – and upsetting lamps, the little innocents! – and quarrelling, and going on generally. O dear, O dear!'

'Well, I'll tell you what I'll do,' said the good engine-driver. 'You're a washerwoman to your trade, say you. Very well, that's that. And I'm an engine-driver, as you well may see, and there's no denying it's terribly dirty work. Uses up a power of shirts, it does, till my missus is fair tired of washing 'em. If you'll wash a few shirts for me when you get home, and send 'em along, I'll give you a ride on my engine. It's against the Company's regulations, but we're not so very particular in these out-of-the-way parts.'

The Toad's misery turned into rapture as he eagerly scrambled up into the cab of the engine. Of course, he had never washed a shirt in his life, and couldn't if he tried and, anyhow, he wasn't going to begin; but he thought: 'when I get safely home to Toad Hall, and have money again, and pockets to put it in, I will send the engine-driver enough to pay for quite a quantity of washing, and that will be the same thing, or better.'

The guard waved his welcome flag, the engine-driver whistled, and the train moved out of the station. As the speed increased, and the Toad could see on either side of him real fields, and trees, and hedges, and cows, and horses, all flying past him, and as he thought how every minute was bringing him nearer to Toad Hall, and sympathetic friends, and money to chink in his pocket, and a soft bed to sleep in, and good things to eat, and praise and admiration at the recital of his adventures and his cleverness, he began to skip up and down and shout and sing snatches of song, to the great astonishment of the engine-driver, who had come across washerwomen before, but never one at all like this.

They had covered many and many a mile, and Toad was already considering what he would have for supper as soon as he got home, when he noticed that the engine-driver, with a puzzled expression on his face, was leaning over the side of the engine and listening hard. 'It's very strange, we're the last train running in this direction tonight, yet I could have sworn that I heard another following us!'

Toad stopped his antics at once. He became grave and depressed, and a dull pain in the lower part of his spine, moving down to his legs, made him want to sit down and try desperately not to think of what might happen.

By this time the moon was shining brightly, and the engine-driver, steadying himself on the coal, could see the line behind them for a long distance. Presently he called out, 'I can see it clearly now! It is an engine, on our rails, coming along at a great speed! It looks as if we are being followed!'

The miserable Toad, crouching in the coal dust, tried hard to think of something to do, with dismal lack of success.

'They are gaining on us fast!' cried the engine-driver. 'And the engine is crowded with the queerest lot of people! Men like ancient warders; policemen in their helmets, waving truncheons; and shabbily dressed men in pot-hats, unmistakable plain clothes detectives even at this distance, waving revolvers and walking sticks; all waving, and all shouting the same thing – "Stop, stop, stop!"'

Then Toad fell on his knees among the coals and, raising his clasped paws in prayer, cried, 'Save me, only save me, dear kind Mr Engine-driver, and I will confess everything! I am not the simple washerwoman I seem to be! I have no children

waiting for me. I am a toad – the well-known and popular Mr Toad; I have just escaped, by my great daring and cleverness, from a dungeon into which my enemies had flung me; and if those fellows on that engine recapture me, it will be chains and bread and water and straw and misery once more for poor, unhappy, innocent Toad!'

The engine driver looked down upon him very sternly, and said, 'Now tell the truth; what were you put in prison for?'

'It was nothing very much,' said poor Toad, blushing deeply, 'I only borrowed a motor-car while the owners were at lunch; they had no need of it at the time. I didn't mean to steal it, really; but people – especially magistrates – take such harsh views of thoughtless and high-spirited actions.'

The engine-driver looked very grave and said, 'I fear that you have been indeed a wicked toad, and by rights I ought to give you up. But you are evidently in trouble and distress, so I will not desert you. I don't hold with motor-cars, for one thing; and I don't hold with being ordered about by policemen when I'm on my own engine, for another. And the sight of an animal in tears always makes me feel soft-hearted. So cheer up, Toad! I'll do my best. We may beat them yet!'

They piled on more coals, shovelling furiously; the furnace roared, the sparks flew, the engine leapt and swung, but still the other engine slowly gained. The engine-driver, with a sign, wiped his brow with a rag, and said, 'I'm afraid it's no good, Toad. You see, they are running light, and they have the better engine. There's just one thing left for us to do, and it's your only chance, so listen very carefully to what I tell you. A short way ahead of us is a long tunnel, and on the other side of that the line passes through a thick wood. Now, I will lying dark and helpful upon either side of the line. The driver shut off steam and put on brakes, the Toad got down on the step, and as the train slowed down to almost a walking pace he heard the driver call out, 'Now, jump!'

Toad jumped, rolled down a short bank, picked himself up unhurt, scrambled into the wood and hid.

Peeping out, he saw his train get up speed again and disappear at a great pace. Then out of the tunnel burst the other engine, roaring and whistling, her motley crew waving their various weapons and shouting, 'Stop! stop! stop!' When they were past, the Toad had a hearty laugh – for the first time since he was thrown into prison.

But he soon stopped laughing when he came to consider that it was now very late and dark and cold, and he was in an unknown wood, with no money and no chance of supper, and still far from friends and home; and the dead silence of every-thing, after the roar and rattle of the train, was something of a shock. He dared not leave the shelter of the trees, so he marched into the wood, with the idea of leaving the railway as far as possible behind him.

At last, cold, hungry, and tired out, he sought the shelter of a hollow tree, where with branches and dead leaves, he made himself as comfortable a bed as he could, and slept soundly till the morning.

put on all the speed I can while we are running through the tunnel, but the other fellows will slow down a bit, for fear of an accident. When we are through, I will shut off steam and put on brakes as hard as I can, and the moment it's safe to do so you must jump and hide in the wood, before they get through the tunnel and see you. Then I will go full speed ahead again, and they can chase *me* if they like, for as long as they like, and as far as they like. Now mind and be ready to jump when I tell you!'

They piled on more coals, and the train shot into the tunnel, and the engine rushed and roared and rattled, till at last they shot out at the other end into fresh air and the peaceful moonlight, and saw the wood

CHAPTER 6

THE FURTHER
ADVENTURES OF TOAD

The front door of the hollow tree faced eastwards, so
Toad was called at an early hour, partly by the bright sunlight streaming in on him, partly by the coldness of his toes,
which made him dream that he was at home in bed in his
own handsome room with Tudor windows, on a cold winter's night, and his bedclothes had got up, grumbling and
protesting they couldn't stand the cold any longer, and had
run downstairs to the kitchen fire to warm themselves.

Sitting up, he rubbed his eyes first and his complaining
toes next, wondered for a moment where he was, looking
round for familiar stone wall and little barred window;
then, with a leap of the heart, remembered everything – his
escape, his flight, his pursuit; remembered, first and best
thing of all, that he was free!

Free! The word and the thought alone were worth fifty
blankets. He was warm from end to end as he thought of
the world outside, waiting eagerly for him to make his tri-
umphal entrance, ready to serve him and play up to him.
He shook himself and combed the dry leaves out of this
hair with his fingers; and, his grooming complete, marched
forth into the comfortable morning sun, cold but confi-
dent, hungry but hopeful, all nervous terrors of yesterday
dispelled by rest and sleep and heartening sunshine.

The road was presently joined by a canal which ambled

along by its side. Round a bend in the canal came plodding a solitary horse, stooping forward as if in anxious thought. From rope traces attached to his collar stretched a long line, taut, but dipping with his stride, the further part of it dripping pearly drops. Toad let the horse pass, and stood waiting for what the fates were sending him.

With a pleasant swirl of quiet water at its blunt bow the barge slid up alongside of him, its gaily painted gunwale level with the towing path, its sole occupant a big stout woman wearing a linen sun bonnet, one brawny arm laid along the tiller.

'A nice morning, ma'am!' she remarked to Toad, as she drew up level with him.

'I dare say it is, ma'am!' responded Toad politely, as he walked along the tow path abreast of her. 'I dare say it is a nice morning to them that's not in sore trouble, like what I am. Here's my married daughter, she sends off to me post haste to come to her at once; so off I comes, not knowing what may be happening or going to happen, but fearing the worst, as you will understand, ma'am, if you're a mother, too. And I've left my business to look after itself – I'm in the washing and laundering line, you must know, ma'am – and I've left my young children to look after themselves, and I've lost all my money, and lost my way, and as for what may be happening to my married daughter, why, I don't like to think of it, ma'am!'

'Where might your married daughter be living, ma'am?' asked the barge-woman.

'She lives near to the river, ma'am,' replied Toad. 'Close to a fine house called Toad Hall, that's somewheres hereabouts. Perhaps you may have heard of it.'

'Toad Hall? Why, I'm going that way myself,' replied the barge-woman. 'This canal joins the river some miles further on, a little above Toad Hall; and then it's an easy walk. You come along in the barge with me, and I'll give you a lift.'

She steered the barge close to the bank, and Toad, with humble thanks, stepped lightly on board and sat down with great satisfaction. 'Toad's luck again!' thought he. 'I always come out on top!'

'So you're in the washing business, ma'am?' said the barge-woman politely, as they glided along. 'And a very good business you've got too, I dare say, if I'm not making too free in saying so.'

'Finest business in the whole country,' said Toad airily. 'All the gentry come to me – wouldn't go to any one else if they were paid, they know me so well. You see, I understand my work thoroughly, and attend to it all myself. Washing, ironing, clear starching, making up gents' fine shirts for evening wear – everything's done under my own eye!'

'But surely you don't do all that work yourself, ma'am?' asked the barge-woman respectfully.

'O, I have girls,' said Toad lightly: 'twenty girls or thereabouts, always at work. But you know what *girls* are, ma'am! Nasty little hussies, that's what I call 'em!'

'So do I, too,' said the barge-woman with great heartiness. 'But I dare say you set yours to rights, the lazy things! And are you very fond of washing?'

'I love it,' said Toad. 'I simply dote on it. Never so happy as when I've got both arms in the wash tub. But, then, it comes so easy to me! No trouble at all! A real pleasure, I assure you, ma'am!'

'What a bit of luck, meeting you!' said the barge-woman thoughtfully. 'A regular piece of good fortune for both of us!'

'Why, what do you mean?' asked Toad nervously.

'Well, look at me, now,' replied the barge-woman. 'I like washing, too, just the same as you do; and for that matter, whether I like it or not I have got to do all my own, naturally, moving about as I do. Now my husband, he's such a fellow for shirking his work and leaving the barge to me, that never a moment do I get for seeing to my own affairs.

'By rights he ought to be here now, either steering or attending to the horse, though luckily the horse has sense enough to attend to himself. Instead of which, he's gone off with the dog, to see if they can't pick up a rabbit for dinner somewhere. Says he'll catch me up at the next lock. Well, that's as may be – I don't trust him, once he gets off with that dog, who's worse than he is. But, meantime, how am I to get on with my washing?'

'O, never mind about the washing,' said Toad, not liking the subject. 'Try and fix your mind on that rabbit. A nice fat young rabbit, I'll be bound. Got any onions?'

'I can't fix my mind on anything but my washing,' said the barge-woman, 'and I wonder you can be talking of rabbits, with such a joyful prospect before you. There's a heap of things of mine that you'll find in a corner of the cabin. If you'll just take one or two of the most necessary sort – I won't venture to describe them to a lady like you, but you'll recognise 'em at a glance – and put them through the wash tub as we go along, why, it'll be a pleasure to you, as you rightly say, and a real help to me.'

'Here, you let me steer!' said Toad, now thoroughly frightened, 'and then you can get on with your washing your own way. I might spoil your things, or not do 'em as you like. I'm more used to gentlemen's things myself. It's my special line.'

'Let you steer?' replied the barge-woman, laughing. 'It takes some practice to steer a barge properly. No, you shall do the washing you are so fond of, and I'll stick to the steering that I understand. Don't try and deprive me of the pleasure of giving you a treat!'

Toad was fairly cornered. He looked for escape this way and that, saw that he was too far from the bank for a flying leap, and sullenly resigned himself to his fate. 'If it comes to that,' he thought in desperation, 'I suppose any fool can wash!'

He fetched tub, soap, and other necessaries from the cabin, selected a few garments at random, tried to recollect what he had seen in casual glances through laundry windows, and set to.

A long half-hour passed, and every minute of it saw Toad getting crosser and crosser. Nothing that he could do to the things seemed to please them or do them good. Once or twice he looked nervously over his shoulder at the barge-woman, but she appeared to be gazing out in front of her, busy with her steering. His back ached badly, and he noticed with dismay that his paws were beginning to get all crinkly. Now Toad was very proud of his paws. He muttered under his breath words that should never pass the lips of either washerwomen or toads; and lost the soap, for the fiftieth

time. A burst of laughter made him straighten himself and look round. The barge-woman was leaning back and laughing, till the tears ran down her cheeks.

'I've been watching you all the time,' she gasped. 'I thought you must be a humbug all along, from the conceited way you talked. Pretty washerwoman you are! Never washed so much as a dish cloth in your life, I'd say!'

Toad's temper, which had been simmering viciously for some time, now fairly boiled over, and he lost all control of himself. 'You common, low, *fat* barge-woman!' he shouted, 'don't you dare to talk to your betters like that! Washerwoman indeed! I would have you to know that I am a toad, a very well-known, respected, distinguished toad! I may be under a bit of a cloud at present, but I will not be laughed at by a barge-woman!'

The woman moved nearer to him and peered under his bonnet keenly and closely. 'Why, so you are!' she cried. 'Well, I never! A horrid, nasty, crawly toad! And in my nice clean barge, too! Now that is a thing that I will *not* have.'

She let go of the tiller for a moment. One

big mottled arm shot out and caught Toad by a fore-leg, while the other gripped him fast by a hind-leg. Then the world turned suddenly upside down, the barge seemed to flit lightly across the sky, the wind whistled in his ears, and Toad found himself flying through the air, revolving rapidly as he went.

The water, when he eventually reached it with a loud splash, proved quite cold enough for his taste, though its chill was not sufficient to quell his proud spirit, or slake the heat of his furious temper. He rose to the surface spluttering, and when he had wiped the duckweed out of his eyes the first thing he saw was the fat barge-woman looking back at him over the stern of the barge and laughing; and he vowed, as he coughed and choked, to be even with her.

He struck out for the shore, but the cotton gown greatly impeded his efforts, and when at length he touched land he found it hard to climb up the steep bank.

He had to take a minute or two's rest to recover his breath; then, gathering his wet skirts well over his arms, he started to run after the barge as fast as his legs would carry him, wild with indignation, thirsting for revenge.

The barge-woman was still laughing when he drew up level with her. 'Put your-self through your mangle, washerwoman,' she called out, 'and iron your face and crimp it, and you'll pass for quite a decent looking toad!'

Toad never paused to reply. Revenge was what he wanted, not an exchange of words, though he had a thing or two in his mind that he would have liked to say. He saw what he wanted ahead of him. Running swiftly on he overtook the horse, unfastened the tow-rope and cast off, jumped lightly on the horse's back, and urged it to a gallop by kicking it hard in the sides. He steered for the open country, leaving the tow-path, and swinging his steed down a bumpy lane. Once he looked back, and saw that the barge had run aground on the other side of the canal, and the barge woman was waving her arms wildly and shouting, 'Stop, stop, stop!'

'I've heard that song before,' said Toad, laughing, as he continued to spur his steed onward in its wild gallop.

The barge-horse was not capable of any very sustained effort, and its gallop soon subsided into a trot, and its trot into an easy walk; but Toad was quite contented with this, knowing that he, at any rate, was moving, and the barge was not.

He had travelled some miles when he came to a wide common, dotted with patches of gorse and bramble as far as he could see. Near him stood a dingy gipsy caravan, and beside it a man was sitting on a bucket turned upside down, very busy smoking and staring into the wide world.

A fire of sticks was burning near by, and over the fire hung an iron pot, and out of that pot came forth bubblings and gurglings. Also smells – warm, rich, and varied smells – that twined and twisted and wreathed themselves at last into one complete, perfect smell. Toad now knew well that he had not been really hungry before. What he had felt earlier in the day had been nothing. This was the real thing at last, and no mistake; and it would have to be dealt with speedily, too, or there would be trouble for somebody or something.

Presently the gipsy took his pipe out of his mouth and remarked in a careless way, 'Want to sell that there horse of yours?'

Toad was completely taken aback. But the gypsy's suggestion seemed to smooth the way towards the two things he wanted so badly – ready money and a solid breakfast.

He managed to say, 'Look here, this fine horse of mine is a cut above you altogether. He's a blood horse, he is, partly; not the part you see, of course – another part. No, it's not to be thought of for a moment. All the same, how much would you offer me for this beautiful horse of mine?'

The gypsy looked the horse over, and then he looked Toad over with equal care, and looked at the horse again. 'Shillin' a leg,' he said briefly, and turned away.

'A shilling a leg?' cried Toad, 'Why, that comes to exactly four shillings, and no more. O no; I could not think of accepting four shillings for this beautiful young horse of mine.'

'Well,' said the gypsy, 'I'll tell you what I will do. I'll make it five shillings, and that's three-and-six-pence more than the animal's worth. And that's my last word.'

Then Toad sat and pondered long and deeply. For he was hungry and quite penniless, and still some way – he knew not how far – from home. At last he said firmly, 'Look here, gypsy! I tell you what we will do; and this is my last word. You shall hand me over six shillings and sixpence, cash down; and in addition you shall give me as much breakfast as I can possibly eat, at one sitting of course, out of that iron pot of yours.

'In return, I will make over to you my spirited young horse, with all the beautiful harness and trappings that are on him, freely thrown in.'

The gypsy grumbled, but in the end he took a dirty canvas bag out of the depths of his trouser pocket, and counted six shillings and sixpence into Toad's paw. Then he disappeared into the caravan, and returned with a large iron plate and a knife, fork, and spoon. He tilted up the pot, and a glorious stream of hot stew gurgled into the plate. Toad took the plate on his lap, almost crying, and stuffed, and kept asking for more. He thought that he had never eaten so good a breakfast in all his life.

When Toad had taken as much stew on board as he thought he could possibly hold, he got up and said goodbye to the gypsy, and took an affectionate farewell of the horse; and the gypsy, who knew the riverside well, gave him directions which way to go, and he set forth on his travels again in the best possible spirits. He was, indeed, a very different Toad from the animal of an hour ago. The sun was shinning brightly, his wet clothes were quite dry again, he had money in his pockets once more, he was nearing home and friends and safety, and, most and best of all, he had had a substantial meal, hot and nourishing, and felt big, and strong, and careless, and self-confident.

As he tramped along gaily, he thought of his adventures and escapes, and how when things seemed at their worst he had always managed to find a way out; and his pride and conceit began to swell within him. 'Ho, ho!' he said to himself as he marched along with his chin in the air, 'what a clever Toad I am! There is surely no animal equal to me for cleverness in the whole world! My enemies shut me up in prison, encircled by sentries, watched night and day by warders; I walk out through them all, by sheer ability and courage. They pursue me with engines, and policemen, and revolvers; I snap my fingers at them, and vanish, laughing, into space. I am, unfortunately, thrown into a canal by a woman, fat of body and very evil-minded. What of it? I swim ashore, I seize her horse, I ride off in triumph, and I sell the horse for a whole pocketful of money and an excellent breakfast! Ho, ho! I am The Toad, the handsome, the popular, the successful Toad!' He got so puffed up with conceit that he made up a song as he walked in praise of himself, and sang it at the top of his voice, though there was no one to hear it but him. It was perhaps the most conceited song that any animal ever composed.

He sang as he walked, and he walked as he sang, and got more inflated every minute. But his pride was shortly to have a severe fall.

After some miles of country lanes he reached the high road, and as he turned into it and glanced along its white length, he saw approaching him a speck that turned into a dot and then into a blob, and then into something very familiar; and a double note of warning, only too well known, fell on his delighted ear.

'This is something like!' said the excited Toad. 'This is real life again, this is once more the great world from which I have been missed so long! I will hail them, my brothers of the wheel, and pitch them a yarn; and they will give me a lift, of course, and then I will talk to them some more; and, perhaps, with luck, it may even end in my driving up to Toad Hall in a motor-car! That will be one in the eye for Badger!'

He stepped confidently out into the road to hail the motor-car, which came along at an easy pace, slowing down as it neared the lane; when suddenly he became very pale, his heart turned to water, his knees shook, and he doubled up and collapsed with a sickening pain in his insides. And well he might, the unhappy animal; for the approaching car was the very one he had stolen out of the yard of the Red Lion Hotel on that fatal day when all his troubles began! And the people in it were the very same people he had sat and watched at lunch in the coffee room!

He sank down in a shabby, miserable heap in the road, murmuring to himself in his despair, 'It's all up! It's all over now! Chains and policemen again! Prison again!

Dry bread and water again! O, what a fool I have been! What did I want to go strutting about the country for, singing conceited songs, and hailing people in broad daylight on the high road, instead of hiding till nightfall and slipping home quietly by back ways! O hapless Toad! O ill-fated animal!'

The terrible motor-car drew slowly nearer and nearer, till at last he heard it stop just short of him. Two gentlemen got out and walked round the trembling heap of crumpled misery lying in the road, and one of them said, 'O dear! this is very sad! Here is a poor old thing – a washerwoman apparently – who has fainted in the road! Perhaps she is overcome by the heat, poor creature; or possibly she has not had any food today. Let us lift her into the car and take her to the nearest village, where doubtless she has friends.'

They tenderly lifted Toad into the motor-car and propped him up with soft cushions, and went on their way.

When Toad heard them talk in so kind and sympathetic a manner, he knew that he was not recognised, his courage began to revive, and he cautiously opened first one eye and then the other.

'Look!' said one of the gentlemen, 'she is better already. The fresh air is doing her good. How do you feel now, ma'am?'

'Thank you kindly, sir,' said Toad in a feeble voice, 'I'm feeling a great deal better!'

'That's right,' said the gentleman. 'Now keep quite still, and, above all, don't try to talk.'

'I won't,' said Toad. 'I was only thinking, if I might sit on the front seat there, beside the driver, where I could get the fresh air full in my face, I should soon be all right again.'

'What a very sensible woman!' said the gentleman. 'Of course you shall.' So they carefully helped Toad into the front seat beside the driver, and on they went once more.

Toad was almost himself again by now. He sat up, looked about him, and tried to be calm.

'It is fate!' he said to himself. He turned to the driver at his side. 'Please, sir,' he said, 'I wish you would kindly let me try and drive the car for a little. I've been watching you carefully, and it looks so easy and so interesting, and I should like to be able to tell my friends that once I had driven a motor-car!'

The driver laughed at the proposal, so heartily that the gentleman asked what the matter was. When he heard, he said, to Toad's delight, 'Bravo, ma'am! I like your spirit. Let her have a try, and look after her. She won't do any harm.'

Toad eagerly scrambled into the driver's seat, took the steering wheel in his hands, listened with affected humility to the instructions given him, and very slowly and carefully, he set the car in motion.

The gentlemen behind clapped their hands and applauded, and Toad heard them saying, 'How well she does it! Fancy a washerwoman driving a car as well as that, the first time!'

Toad went a little faster; then faster still, and faster.

He heard the gentleman call out warningly, 'Be careful, washerwoman!' This annoyed him, and he began to lose his head.

The driver tried to interfere, but he pinned him down in his seat with one elbow, and put on full speed. The rush of air in his face, the hum of the engine, and the light jump of the car beneath him made him very excited.

'Washerwoman, indeed!' he shouted recklessly. 'Ho, ho! I am the Toad, the motor-car snatcher, the prison-breaker, the Toad who always escapes! Sit still, and you shall know what driving really is, for you are in the hands of the famous, the skilful, the entirely fearless Toad!'

With a cry of horror the whole party rose and flung themselves on him. 'Seize him!' they cried, 'seize the Toad, the wicked animal who stole our motor-car! Bind him, chain him, drag him to the nearest police station! Down with the desperate and dangerous Toad!'

Alas! they should have thought, they should have remembered to stop the motor-car somehow before playing any pranks of that sort. With a half-turn of the wheel the Toad sent the car crashing through the low hedge that ran along the roadside. One mighty bound, a violent shock, and the wheels of the car were churning up the thick mud of a horse-pond.

Toad found himself flying through the air with the strong upward rush and delicate curve of a swallow. He liked the motion, and was just beginning to wonder whether it would go on, when he landed on his back with a thump, in the soft rich grass of a meadow. Sitting up, he could just see the motor-car in the pond, nearly submerged; the gentlemen and the driver, weighed down by their long coats, were floundering helplessly in the water.

He picked himself up rapidly and set off running across country as hard as he could, scrambling through hedges, jumping ditches, pounding across fields, till he was breathless and weary, and had to settle down into an easy walk. When he had recovered his breath somewhat, and was able to think calmly, he began to giggle, and from giggling he took to laughing, and he laughed till he had to sit down under a hedge.

'Ho, ho!' he cried. 'Toad again! Toad, as usual comes out on top!

'O, how clever I am! How clever, how clever, how very clev–'

A slight noise at a distance behind him made him turn his head and look. O horror! O misery! O despair!

About two fields off, a chauffeur in his leather gaiters and two large rural policemen were visible, running towards him as hard as they could go!

Poor Toad sprang to his feet and pelted away again, his heart in his mouth. 'O my!' he gasped, as he panted along, 'what a fool I am! What a conceited and heedless fool! Swaggering again! Shouting and singing songs again! Sitting still and gassing again! O my! O my! O my!'

He glanced back, and saw to his dismay that they were gaining on him. On he ran desperately, but kept looking back, and saw that they still gained steadily. He did his best, but he was a fat animal, and his legs were short, and still they gained. He could hear them close behind him now.

Ceasing to heed where he was going, he struggled on blindly and wildly, looking back over his shoulder at the now triumphant enemy, when suddenly the earth failed under his feet, he grasped at the air, and, splash! he found himself head over ears in deep water, rapid water, water that bore him along with a force he could not contend with; and he knew that in his blind panic he had run straight into the river!

He rose to the surface and tried to grasp the reeds and the rushes that grew along the water's edge close under the bank, but the stream was so strong that it tore them out of his hands. 'O my!' gasped poor Toad, 'if ever I steal a motor-car again! If ever I sing another conceited song' – then down he went, and came up breathless and spluttering.

Presently he saw that he was approaching a big dark hole in the bank, just above his head, and as the stream bore him past he reached up with a paw and caught hold of the edge and held on. Then slowly and with difficulty he drew himself up out of the water, till at last he was able to rest his elbows on the edge of the hole. There he remained for some minutes, puffing and panting, for he was quite exhausted.

As he sighed and blew and stared before him into the dark hole, some bright small thing shone and twinkled in its depths, moving towards him. As it approached, a face grew up gradually around it, and it was a familiar face!

Brown and small, with whiskers.

Grave and round, with neat ears and silky hair.

It was the Water Rat!

CHAPTER 7

'LIKE SUMMER TEMPESTS CAME HIS TEARS'

The Rat put out a neat little brown paw, gripped Toad firmly by the scruff of the neck, and gave a great hoist and a pull; and the water-logged Toad came up slowly but surely over the edge of the hole, till at last he stood safe and sound in the hall, streaked with mud and weed to be sure, and with the water streaming off him, but happy and high-spirited as of old, now that he found himself once more in the house of a friend.

'O Ratty!' he cried. 'I've been through such times since I saw you last, you can't think! Such trials, such sufferings, and all so nobly borne! Then such escapes, such disguises, such tricks, and all so cleverly planned and carried out! Just hold on till I tell you – '

'Toad,' said the Water Rat, gravely and firmly, 'you go off upstairs at once, and take off that old cotton rag that looks as if it might formerly have belonged to some washerwoman, and clean yourself thoroughly, and put on some of my clothes, and try and come down looking like a gentleman if you can; for a more shabby, bedraggled, disreputable-looking object than you are I never set eyes on in my whole life! Now, stop swaggering and arguing, and be off! I'll have something to say to you later!'

Toad was at first inclined to stop and do some talking back at him. He had had enough of being ordered about when he was in prison. However, he caught sight of himself in the mirror over the hat-stand, with the black bonnet perched rakishly over one eye, and he changed his mind and went very quickly and humbly upstairs to the Rat's dressing-room. There he had a thorough wash and brush-up, changed his clothes, and stood for a long time before the glass, looking at himself with pride and pleasure, and thinking what utter idiots all the people must have been to have ever mistaken him for one moment for a washerwoman.

By the time he came down again lunch was on the table, and very glad Toad was to see it, for he had been through some trying experiences and had taken much hard exercise since the excellent breakfast provided for him by the gipsy. While they ate Toad told the Rat all his adventures, dwelling chiefly on his own cleverness, and presence of mind in emergencies, and cunning in tight places. But the more he talked and boasted, the more grave and silent the Rat became.

When at last Toad had talked himself to a standstill, there was silence for a while; and then the Rat said, 'Now, Toady, I don't want to give you pain, after all you've been through already; but, seriously, don't you see what an awful idiot you've been making of yourself? And all because you must needs to go and steal a motor-car. You know that you've never had anything but trouble from motor-cars from the moment you first set eyes on one. But if you *will* be mixed up with them – as you generally are, five minutes after you've started – why *steal* them? When are you going to be sensible, and think of your friends, and try and be a credit to them? Do you suppose it's any pleasure to me, for instance, to hear animals saying, as I go about, that I'm the fellow that keeps company with gaol-birds?'

Now, it was a very comfortable point in Toad's character that he was a thoroughly good-hearted animal, and never minded being told off by those who were his real friends. And even when most set upon a thing, he was always able to see the other side of the question. So although, while the Rat was talking so seriously, he kept making strange sounds resembling stifled snorts, or the opening of soda-water bottles, yet when the Rat had quite finished, he heaved a deep sigh and said, very nicely and humbly, 'Quite right, Ratty! How *sound* you always are! Yes, I've been a conceited old fool, I can quite see that; but now I'm going to be a good Toad, and not do it any more. We'll have our coffee, and a smoke, and a quiet chat, and then I'm going to stroll gently down to Toad Hall, and get into clothes of my own, and set things going again on the old lines.'

'Stroll gently down to Toad Hall?' cried the Rat, greatly excited. 'What are you talking about? Do you mean to say you haven't *heard*?'

'Heard what?' said Toad, turning rather pale. 'Go on, Ratty! Quick! Don't spare me! What haven't I heard?'

'Do you mean to tell me,' shouted the Rat, thumping with his little fist upon the table, 'that you've heard nothing about the Stoats and Weasels?'

'What, the Wild Wooders?' cried Toad, trembling in every limb. 'No, not a word! What have they been doing?'

'–And how they've been and taken Toad Hall?' continued the Rat. Toad leaned his elbows on the table, and his chin on his paws; and a large tear welled up in each of his eyes, overflowed and splashed on the table, plop! plop!

'Go on, Ratty,' he murmured presently. 'Tell me all. The worst is over. I am an animal again. I can bear it.'

'When you – got – into that – that – trouble of yours,' said the Rat slowly and impressively; 'I mean, when you – disappeared for a time, over that misunderstanding about a – a machine, you know.'

Toad merely nodded.

'Well, it was a good deal talked about down here, naturally,' continued the Rat, 'not only along the riverside, but even in the Wild Wood. Animals took sides, as always happens. The Wild Wood animals said hard things, and served you right, and it was time this sort of thing stopped. And they went about saying you were done for this time! You would never come back again, never, never!'

Toad nodded once more, keeping silence.

'That's the sort of little beasts they are,' the Rat went on. 'But Mole and Badger, they stuck out, through thick and thin, that you would come back again soon, somehow. They didn't know exactly how, but somehow!'

Toad began to sit up in his chair again, and to smirk a little.

'They argued from history,' continued the Rat. 'They said that no criminal laws had ever been known to win the day against cheek and a good case such as yours, combined with the power of a deep purse. So they arranged to move their things into Toad Hall, and sleep there, and keep it aired, and have it all ready for you when you turned up. Now I come to the most painful and tragic part of my own story. One dark night – it was a *very* dark night, and blowing hard, too, and raining simply cats and dogs – a band of weasels, armed to the teeth, crept silently up the carriage-drive to the front entrance. At the same time, a body of desperate ferrets, advancing

through the kitchen garden, possessed themselves of the back yard and offices; while a company of skirmishing stoats who stopped at nothing occupied the conservatory and the billiard room, and held the French windows opening on to the lawn.

'The Mole and the Badger were sitting by the fire in the smoking room, telling stories and suspecting nothing, for it wasn't a night for any animals to be out in, when those bloodthirsty villains broke down the doors and rushed in upon them from every side. They made the best fight they could, but what was the good? They were unarmed, and taken by surprise, and what can two animals do against hundreds? They took and beat them severely with sticks, those two poor faithful creatures, and turned them out into the cold and the wet, with many insulting and uncalled for remarks!'

Here the unfeeling Toad broke into a snigger, and then pulled himself together and tried to look particularly solemn.

'And the Wild Wooders have been living in Toad Hall ever since,' continued the Rat. 'And they're telling the tradespeople and everybody that they've come to stay for good.'

brought his gun up to his shoulder. Toad dropped flat in the road, and Bang! a bullet whistled over his head.

The startled Toad scrambled to his feet and scampered off down the road as hard as he could; and as he ran he heard the ferret laughing, and other horrid thin little laughs taking it up and carrying on the sound.

He went back, very crestfallen, and told the Water Rat.

'*What* did I tell you?' said the Rat. 'It's no good. They've got sentries posted, and they are all armed. You must just wait.'

'Ratty! I see that I have been a headstrong and a wilful Toad! Henceforth, believe me, I will be humble and submissive, and will take no action without your kind advice and full approval!'

'If that is really so,' said the good-natured Rat, 'then my advice to you is, considering the lateness of the hour, to sit down and have your supper, which will be on the table in a minute, and be very patient. For I am convinced that we can do nothing until we have seen the Mole and the Badger, and heard their latest news, and held conference and taken their advice in this difficult matter.'

'O, ah, yes, of course, the Mole and the Badger,' said Toad lightly. 'What's become of them, the dear fellows? I had forgotten all about them.'

'Well may you ask!' said the Rat sharply. 'While you were riding about the country in expensive motor-cars, and galloping proudly on blood horses, and breakfasting on the fat of the land, those two poor devoted animals have been camping out in the open, in every sort of weather, living very rough by day and lying very hard by night; watching over your house, keeping a constant eye on the stoats and the weasels, scheming and planning how to get your property back for you. You don't deserve to have such true and loyal friends, Toad, you don't really. Some day, when it's too late, you'll be sorry

'O, have they!' said Toad, getting up and seizing a stick. 'I'll soon see about that!'

'It's no good, Toad!' called the Rat after him. 'You'd better come back and sit down; you'll only get into trouble.'

But the Toad was off, and there was no holding him. He marched rapidly down the road, his stick over his shoulder, fuming and muttering to himself in his anger, till he got near his front gate, when suddenly there popped up from behind the palings a long yellow ferret with a gun.

'Who comes there?' said the ferret sharply.

'Stuff and nonsense!' said Toad very angrily. 'What do you mean by talking like that to me? Come out of it at once, or I'll–'

The ferret said never a word, but he

you didn't value them more while you had them!'

'I'm an ungrateful beast, I know,' sobbed Toad, shedding bitter tears. 'Let me go out and find them, out into the cold, dark night and share their hardships, and try and prove by – hold on a bit! Surely I heard the chink of dishes on a tray! Supper's here at last, hooray! Come on, Ratty!'

The Rat remembered that poor Toad had been on prison rations for a considerable time, and that large allowances had therefore to be made. He followed him to the table and encouraged him in his gallant efforts to make up for past hardships.

They had just finished their meal and returned to their armchairs, when there came a heavy knock at the door.

Toad was nervous, but the Rat, nodding mysteriously at him, went straight up to the door and opened it, and in walked Mr Badger.

He had all the appearance of one who for some nights had been kept away from home and all its little comforts and conveniences. His shoes were covered with mud, and he was looking very rough and untidy; but then he had never been a very smart man, the Badger, at the best of times. He came solemnly up to Toad, shook him by the paw, and said, 'Welcome home, Toad! Alas! what am I saying? Home, indeed! This is a poor homecoming. Unhappy Toad!' Then he turned his back on him, sat down to the table, drew his chair up, and helped himself to a large slice of cold pie. Presently there came another and a lighter knock. The Rat, with a nod to Toad, went to the door and ushered in the Mole, very shabby and unwashed, with bits of hay and straw sticking in his fur.

'Hooray! Here's old Toad!' cried the Mole, his face beaming. 'Fancy having you back again!' And he began to dance round him. 'We never dreamt you would turn up so soon! Why, you must have managed to escape, you clever Toad!'

The Rat, alarmed, pulled him by the elbow; but it was too late. Toad was puffing and swelling already.

'Clever? O no!' he said. 'I'm not really clever, according to my friends. I've only broken out of the strongest prison in England, that's all! And captured a railway train and escaped on it, that's all!'

'Go on, Toad,' said the Mole, immensely interested.

'Toad, do be quiet, please!' said the Rat. 'And don't you egg him on, Mole, when you know what he is; but please tell us as soon as possible what the position is, and what's best to be done, now that Toad is back at last.'

'The position's about as bad as it can be,' replied the Mole grumpily; 'and as for what's to be done, why, blessed if I know! The Badger and I have been round and round the place, by night and by day; always the same thing. Sentries posted everywhere, guns poked out at us, stones thrown at us; always an animal on the look out, and when they see us, my! how they do laugh! That's what annoys me most!'

'It's a very difficult situation,' said the Rat, reflecting deeply. 'But I think I see now, in the depths of my mind, what Toad really ought to do. I will tell you. He ought to– '

'No, he oughtn't!' shouted the Mole, with his mouth full. 'Nothing of the sort! You don't understand. What he ought to do is, he ought to– '

'Well, I shan't do it, anyway!' cried Toad, getting excited. 'I'm not going to be ordered about by you fellows! It's my house we're talking about, and I know exactly what to do, and I'll tell you.'

'Toad!' the Badger said severely. 'You bad, troublesome little animal! Aren't you ashamed of yourself? What do you think your father, my old friend, would have said if he had been here tonight, and had known of all your goings on?'

Toad, who was on the sofa by this time, with his legs up, rolled over on his face, shaken by sobs of regret.

'There, there!' went on the Badger more kindly. 'Never mind. Stop crying. We're going to let bygones be bygones, and try and turn over a new leaf. But what the Mole says is quite true. The stoats are on guard, at every point, and they make the best guards in the world. It's quite useless to think of attacking the place. They're too strong for us.'

'Then it's all over,' sobbed the Toad, crying into the sofa cushions. 'I shall go and enlist for a soldier, and never see my dear Toad Hall any more!'

'Come, cheer up, Toady!' said the Badger. 'There are more ways of getting back a place than taking it by storm. I haven't said my last word yet. Now I'm going to tell you a great secret.'

Toad sat up slowly and dried his eyes.

'There – is – an – underground – passage,' said the Badger impressively, 'that leads from the river bank quite near here, right up into the middle of Toad Hall.'

'O, nonsense! Badger,' said Toad rather airily. 'You've been listening to some of the yarns they spin in the public houses about here. I know every inch of Toad Hall, inside and out. Nothing of the sort, I do assure you!'

'My young friend,' said the Badger with great severity, 'your father, who was a worthy animal – a lot worthier than some others I know – was a particular friend of mine, and told me a great deal he wouldn't have dreamt of telling you. He discovered that passage – he didn't make it, of course; that was done hundreds of years before he ever came to live there – and he repaired it and cleaned it out, because he thought it might come in useful some day, in case of trouble or danger, and he showed it to me. "Don't let my son know about it," he said. "He's a good boy, but very light and unstable in character, and simply cannot hold his tongue. If he's ever in a real fix, and it would be of use to him, you may tell him about the secret passage, but not before."'

The other animals looked hard at Toad to see how he would take it. Toad was inclined to be sulky at first; but he brightened up immediately, like the good fellow he was.

'Well, well,' he said; 'perhaps I am a bit of a talker. Never Mind. Go on, Badger. How's this passage of yours going to help us?'

'I've found out a thing or two lately,' continued the Badger. 'I got Otter to disguise himself as a sweep and call at the back door with brushes over his shoulder, asking for a job. There's going to be a big banquet tomorrow night. It's somebody's birthday – the Chief Weasel's, I believe – and all the weasels will be gathered together in the dining hall, eating and drinking and laughing and carrying on, suspecting nothing. No guns, no swords, no sticks, no arms, of any sort whatever!'

'But the guards will be posted as usual,' remarked the Rat.

'Exactly,' said the Badger; 'that is my point. The weasels will trust entirely to their excellent guards. And that is where the passage comes in. That very useful tunnel leads right up under the butler's pantry, next to the dining hall!'

'Aha! That squeaky board in the butler's pantry!' said Toad. 'Now I understand it!'

'We shall creep out quietly into the butler's pantry–' cried the Mole.

'–with our pistols and swords and sticks–' shouted the Rat.

'–and rush in upon them,' said the Badger.

'–and whack 'em, and whack 'em, and whack 'em!' cried the Toad, running round and round the room, and jumping over the chairs.

'Very well, then,' said the Badger, resuming his usual dry manner, 'our plan is settled, and there's nothing more for you to argue and squabble about. So, as it's getting very late, all of you go right off to bed at once. We will make all the necessary arrangements in the course of the morning tomorrow.'

Toad, of course, went off to bed dutifully with the rest – he knew better than to refuse – though he was feeling much too excited to sleep. But he had had a long day, with many events crowded into it; and sheets and blankets were very friendly and comforting things, after plain straw, and not too much of it, spread on the stone floor of a draughty cell; and his head had not been many seconds on his pillow before he was snoring happily.

He slept till a late hour next morning, and by the time he got down he found that the other animals had finished their breakfast some time before. The Mole had slipped off somewhere by himself, without telling anyone where he was going. The Badger sat in the armchair, reading the paper, and not concerning himself in the slightest about what was going to happen that very evening. The Rat, on the other hand, was running round the room busily, with his arms full of weapons of every kind, distributing them in four little heaps on the floor, and saying excitedly under his breath, as he ran, 'Here's-a-sword-for-the-Rat, here's-a-sword-for-the-Mole, here's-a-sword-for-the-Toad, here's-a-sword-for-the-Badger! Here's-a-pistol-for-the-Rat, here's-a-pistol-for-the-Mole, here's-a-pistol-for-the-Toad, here's-a-pistol-for-the-Badger!' And so on, while the four little heaps gradually grew and grew.

'That's all very well, Rat,' said the Badger presently, looking at the busy little animal over the edge of his newspaper; 'I'm not blaming you. But just let us once get past the stoats, with those detestable guns of theirs, and I assure you we shan't want any swords or pistols. We four, with our sticks, once we're inside the dining hall, why, we shall clear the floor of all the lot of them in five minutes. I'd have done the whole thing by myself, only I didn't want to deprive you fellows of the fun!'

'It's as well to be on the safe side,' said the Rat reflectively, polishing a pistol-barrel on his sleeve and looking along it.

Presently the Mole came tumbling into the room, evidently very pleased with himself. 'I've been having such fun!' he began at once; 'I've been getting a laugh out of the stoats!'

'I hope you've been very careful, Mole?' said the Rat anxiously.

'I should hope so, too,' said the Mole confidently. 'I got the idea when I went into the kitchen, to see about Toad's breakfast being kept hot for him. I found that old washerwoman-dress that he came home in yesterday, hanging on a towel-horse before the fire. So I put it on, and the bonnet as well, and the shawl, and off I went to Toad Hall, as bold as you please. The sentries were on the look-out, of course, with their guns and their "Who comes there?" and all the rest of their nonsense. "Good morning, gentlemen!" says I, very respectful. "Want any washing done today?"

'They looked at me very proud and stiff and haughty, and said, "Go away, washerwoman! We don't do any washing on duty." "Or any other time?" says I.

Eric Kincaid

'Some of the stoats turned quite pink,' continued the Mole, 'and the sergeant in charge, he said to me, very short, he said, "Now run away, my good woman, run away! Don't keep my men idling and talking on their posts." "Run away?" says I; "it won't be me that'll be running away, in a very short time from now!"'

'O, *Moly*, how could you?' said the Rat, dismayed.

The Badger laid down his paper.

'I could see them pricking up their ears and looking at each other,' went on the Mole; 'and the sergeant said to them, "Never mind her; she doesn't know what she's talking about."'

'"O! don't I?" said I. "Well, let me tell you this. My daughter, she washes for Mr Badger, and that'll show you whether I know what I'm talking about; and you'll know pretty soon, too! A hundred bloodthirsty badgers, armed with rifles, are going to attack Toad Hall this very night, by way of the paddock. Six boat loads of rats with pistols and cutlasses, will come up the river and land in the garden; while a picked body of toads, known as the Die-hards, or the Death-or-glory Toads, will storm the orchard and carry everything before them, yelling for vengeance. There won't be much left of you to wash, by the time they've done with you, unless you clear out while you have the chance!" Then I ran away, and when I was out of sight I hid; and presently I came creeping back along the ditch and took a peep at them through the hedge. They were all as nervous and flustered as could be, running all ways at once, and falling over each other, and every one giving orders to everybody else and not listening; and the sergeant kept sending off parties of stoats to distance parts of the grounds.'

'O, you silly fool, Mole!' cried Toad. 'You've been and spoilt everything!'

'Mole,' said the Badger, in his dry quiet way, 'I can see you have more sense in your little finger than some other animals have in the whole of their fat bodies. You have managed excellently, and I begin to have great hopes of you. Good Mole! Clever Mole!'

The Toad was simply wild with jealousy, more especially as he couldn't make out for the life of him what the Mole had done that was so particularly clever; but, fortunately for him, before he could show temper or expose himself to the Badger's sarcasm, the bell rang for lunch.

It was a simple meal – bacon and broad beans, and a macaroni pudding; and when they had quite done, the Badger settled himself into an armchair, and said, 'Well, we've got our work cut out for us tonight, and it will probably be pretty late before we're quite through with it; so I'm just going to take forty winks, while I can.' And he drew a handkerchief over his face and was soon snoring.

The hard-working Rat at once resumed his preparations, and started running between his four little heaps, muttering, 'Here's-a-belt-for-the-Rat, here's-a-belt-for-the-Mole, here's-a-belt-for-the-Toad, here's-a-belt-for-the-Badger!' and so on, with every fresh item he produced, to which there seemed really no end; so the Mole drew his arm through Toad's, led him out into the open air, shoved him into a wicker chair, and made him tell him all his adventures from beginning to end, which Toad was only too willing to do. The Mole was a good listener, and Toad, with no one to check his statements or to criticise in an unfriendly spirit, rather let himself go. Indeed, much that he related belonged more properly to the category of what-might-have-happened-had-I-only-thought-of-it-in-time-instead-of-ten-minutes-afterwards. Those are always the best adventures; and why should they not be truly ours, as much as the somewhat inadequate things that really come off?

CHAPTER 8
THE RETURN OF THE HERO

When it began to grow dark, the Rat, with an air of excitement and mystery, called them back into the parlour, stood each of them up alongside his little heap, and proceeded to dress them up for the coming expedition. He was very earnest and thoroughgoing about it, and the affair took quite a long time. First, there was a belt to go round each animal, and then a sword to be stuck into each belt, and then a cutlass on the other side to balance it. Then a pair of pistols, a policeman's truncheon, several sets of handcuffs, some bandages and sticking plaster, and a flask and a sandwich case. The Badger laughed and said, 'All right, Ratty! It amuses you and it doesn't hurt me. I'm going to do all I've got to do with this here stick.' But the Rat only said, '*Please*, Badger! You know I shouldn't like you to blame me afterwards and say I had forgotten *anything*!'

When all was quite ready, the Badger took a dark lantern in one paw, grasped his great stick with the other, and said, 'Now then, follow me! Mole first, 'cos I'm very pleased with him; Rat next; Toad last. And look here, Toady! Don't you chatter so much as usual, or you'll be sent back, as sure as fate!'

The Toad was so anxious not to be left out that he took up the lowly position given to him without a murmur, and the animals set off. The Badger led them along by the river for a little way, and then suddenly swung himself over the edge into a hole in the river bank, a little above the water. The Mole and the Rat followed silently, swinging themselves successfully into the hole as they had seen the Badger do; but when it came to Toad's turn, of course he managed to slip and fall into the water with a loud splash and a squeal of alarm. He was hauled out by his friends, rubbed down and wrung out hastily, comforted, and set on his legs; but the Badger was angry, and told him that the very next time he made a fool of himself he would most certainly be left behind.

So at last they were in the secret passage, and the driving-out expedition had really begun!

They groped and shuffled along, with their ears pricked up and their paws on their pistols, till at last the Badger said, 'We ought by now to be pretty nearly under the Hall.'

Then suddenly they heard, far away as it might be, and yet nearly over their heads, a confused murmur of sound, as if people were shouting and cheering and stamping on the floor and hammering on tables. The Toad's nervous terrors all returned, but the Badger only remarked placidly, 'They *are* going it, the weasels!'

The passage now began to slope upwards; they groped onward a little further, and then the noise broke out again, quite distinct this time, and very close above them. 'Ooo-ray-oo-ray-oo-ray-ooray!' they heard, and the stamping of little feet on the floor, and the clinking of glasses as little fists pounded on the table. '*What* a time they're having!' said the Badger. 'Come on!'

They hurried along the passage till it came to a full stop, and they found themselves standing under the trap-door that led up into the butler's pantry.

Such a tremendous noise was going on in the banqueting hall that there was little danger of their being overheard. The Badger said, 'Now, boys, all together!' and the four of them put their shoulders to the trapdoor and heaved it back. Hoisting each other up, they found themselves standing in the pantry, with only a door between them and the banqueting hall, where their enemies were making merry.

The noise, as they emerged from the passage, was simply deafening. At last, as the cheering and hammering slowly subsided, a voice could be made out saying, 'Well, I do not propose to detain you much longer' – (great applause) – 'but before I resume my seat' – (renewed cheering) – 'I should like to say one word about our kind host, Mr Toad. We all know Toad!' – (great laughter) –' *Good* Toad, *modest* Toad, *honest* Toad!' – (shrieks of merriment).

' – Let me sing you a little song,' went on the voice, 'which I have composed on the subject of Toad' – (prolonged applause).

Then the Chief Weasel – for it was he – began in a squeaky voice:

Toad he went a-pleasuring
Gaily down the street –

The Badger drew himself up, took a firm grip of his stick with both paws, glanced round at his comrades, and cried:

'The hour is come! Follow me!'

And flung the door open wide.

What a squealing and a squeaking and a screeching filled the air!

Well might the terrified weasels dive under the tables and spring madly up at the windows! Well might the ferrets rush wildly for the fireplace and get hopelessly jammed in the chimney! Well might tables and chairs be upset, and glass and china be sent crashing on the floor, in the panic of that terrible moment when the four Heroes

Eric Kincaid

straight for the Chief Weasel. They were but four in all, but to the panic-stricken weasels the hall seemed full of monstrous animals, grey, black, brown, and yellow, whooping and flourishing enormous cudgels; and they broke and fled with squeals of terror and dismay, this way and that, through the windows, up the chimney, anywhere to get out of reach of those terrible sticks.

The affair was soon over. Up and down, the whole length of the hall, strode the four friends, whacking with their sticks at every head that showed itself; and in five minutes the room was cleared. Through the broken windows the shrieks of terrified weasels escaping across the lawn were borne faintly to their ears; on the floor lay some dozen or so of the enemy, on whom the Mole was busily engaged in fitting handcuffs. The Badger, resting from his labours, leant on his stick and wiped his honest brow.

'Mole,' he said, 'you're the best of fellows! Just cut along outside and look after those stoat-sentries of yours, and see what they're doing. I've an idea that, thanks to you, we shan't have much trouble from *them* tonight!'

The Mole vanished promptly through a window; and the Badger got the other two to set a table on its legs again, pick up knives and forks and plates and glasses from the muddle on the floor, and see if they could find materials for a supper. 'I want some grub, I do,' he said, in that rather common way he had of speaking. 'Stir your stumps, Toad, and look lively! We've got your house back for you, and you don't offer us so much as a sandwich.'

Toad felt rather hurt that the Badger didn't say pleasant things to him, as he had to the Mole, and tell him what a fine fellow he was, and how splendidly he had fought; for he was rather particularly pleased with himself and the way he had gone for the Chief Weasel and sent him flying across the table with one blow of his stick. But he bustled

strode wrathfully into the room! The mighty Badger, his whiskers bristling, his great cudgel whistling through the air; Mole, black and grim, brandishing his stick and shouting his awful war-cry, 'A Mole! A Mole!' Rat, desperate and determined, his belt bulging with weapons of every age and every variety; Toad, frenzied with excitement and injured pride, swollen to twice his ordinary size, leaping into the air and crying out Toad-whoops that chilled them to the marrow! 'Toad he went a-pleasuring!' he yelled. '*I'll* pleasure 'em!' and he went about, and so did the Rat, and soon they found a cold chicken, a tongue that had hardly been touched, some trifle, and quite a lot of lobster salad; and in the pantry they came upon a basketful of French rolls and any quantity of cheese, butter, and celery. They were just about to sit down when the Mole clambered in through the window, chuckling, with an armful of rifles.

'It's all over,' he reported. 'From what I can make out, as soon as the stoats, who were very nervous and jumpy already, heard the shrieks and yells and the uproar inside the hall, some of them threw down their rifles and fled. The others stood fast for a bit, but when the weasels came rushing out upon them they thought they were betrayed; and the stoats grappled with the weasels, and the weasels fought to get away, and they wrestled and wriggled and punched each other, and rolled over and over, till most of 'em rolled into the river! They've all disappeared by now, one way or another; and I've got their rifles. So that's all right!'

'Excellent and deserving animal!' said the Badger, his mouth full of chicken and trifle.

Then the Mole pulled his chair up to the table, and pitched into the cold tongue; and Toad, like the gentleman he was, put all his jealousy from him, and said heartily, 'Thank you kindly, dear Mole, for all your pains and trouble tonight, and especially for your cleverness this morning!' The Badger was pleased at that, and said, 'There spoke my brave Toad!' So they finished their supper in great joy and contentment, and presently retired to rest between clean sheets, safe in Toad's ancestral home, won back by great courage, perfect strategy, and a proper handling of sticks.

The following morning, Toad, who had overslept as usual, came down to breakfast disgracefully late, and found on the table a certain quantity of egg-shells, some fragments of cold and leathery toast, a coffee-

pot three-quarters empty, and really very little else; which did not tend to improve his temper, considering that, after all, it was his own house. The Badger, who was in an armchair and deep in the morning paper, merely looked up and nodded when Toad entered the room. So Toad sat down and made the best breakfast he could, merely observing to himself that he would get square with the others sooner or later. When he had nearly finished, the Badger looked up and remarked rather shortly: 'I'm sorry, Toad, but I'm afraid there's a heavy morning's work in front of you. You see, we really ought to have a banquet at once, to celebrate this affair. It's expected of you – in fact, it's the rule.'

'O, all right!' said the Toad readily.

'The invitations will have to be written and got off at once, and you've got to write 'em,' the Badger continued. 'Now, sit down at that table and write invitations to all our friends, and if you stick to it we shall get them out before lunch. And I'll lend a hand, too. I'll order the banquet.'

'What!' cried Toad, dismayed. 'Me stop indoors and write a lot of rotten letters on a fine morning like this, when I want to go around my property, and set everything and everybody to rights, and swagger about and enjoy myself! Certainly not! I'll be – I'll see you – stop a minute, though! Why, of course, dear Badger! What is my pleasure or convenience compared with that of others! You wish it done, and it shall be done.'

The Badger looked at him suspiciously, but Toad's frank, open face made it difficult to suggest any unworthy motive in this change of attitude. He left the room in the direction of the kitchen, and as soon as the door had closed behind him, Toad hurried to the writing table. A fine idea had occurred to him while he was talking. He *would* write the invitations; and he would take care to mention the leading part he had taken in the fight, and how he had laid the Chief Weasel flat; and he would hint at his adventures, and what a career of triumph he had to tell about; and on the first page he would give a sort of program of entertainment for the evening – something like this, as he sketched it out in his head:

SPEECH BY TOAD
(There will be other speeches by Toad during the evening)

ADDRESS BY TOAD

SYNOPSIS — Our Prison system — The Water-ways of Old England — Horse dealing, and how to deal — Property, its Rights and its duties — Back to the Land — A Typical English Squire

SONG BY TOAD
(*Composed by himself*)

OTHER COMPOSITIONS BY TOAD
will be sung in the course of the evening by the . . . COMPOSER

The idea pleased him mightily, and he worked very hard and got all the letters finished by noon, at which hour it was reported to him that there was a small and rather bedraggled weasel at the door, asking timidly whether he could be of any service to the gentlemen. Toad swaggered out and found it was one of the prisoners of the previous evening, very respectful and eager to please. He patted him on the head, shoved the bundle of invitations into his paw, and told him to go along quickly and deliver them as fast as he could, and if he liked to come back again in the evening perhaps there might be a shilling for him, or again, perhaps there mightn't; and the poor weasel seemed really quite grateful, and hurried off eagerly to do his mission.

When the other animals came back to lunch after a morning on the river, the Mole, feeling somewhat guilty, looked doubtfully at Toad, expecting to find him sulky or depressed. Instead, he was so uppish and inflated that the Mole began to suspect something; while the Rat and the Badger exchanged knowing glances.

As soon as the meal was over, Toad thrust his paws deep into his trouser pockets and remarked casually, 'Well, look after yourselves, you fellows! Ask for anything you want!' and was swaggering off in the direction of the garden where he wanted to think out an idea or two for his coming speeches, when the Rat caught him by the arm.

Toad rather suspected what he was after, and did his best to get away; but when the Badger took him firmly by the other arm he began to see that the game was up. The two animals took him between them into the small smoking room that opened out of the entrance hall, shut the door, and put him into a chair.

'Now, look here, Toad,' said the Rat. 'It's about this banquet, and very sorry I am to have to speak to you like this. But we want you to understand clearly, once and for all,

that there are going to be no speeches and no songs. Try and grasp the fact that on this occasion we're not arguing with you; we're just telling you.'

Toad saw that he was trapped. They understood him, they saw through him, they had got ahead of him. His pleasant dream was shattered. 'Can't I sing them just one little song?' he pleaded.

'No, not one little song,' replied the Rat firmly, though his heart bled as he noticed the trembling lip of the poor Toad. 'It's no good, Toady; you know well that your songs are all conceit and boasting and vanity; and your speeches are all self-praise and – and – well, and gross exaggeration and – and–'

'And gas,' put in the Badger, in his common way.

'It's for your own good, Toady,' went on the Rat. 'You know you must turn over a new leaf sooner or later, and now seems a splendid time to begin; a sort of turning-point in your career. Please don't think that saying all this doesn't hurt me more than it hurts you.'

Toad remained a long while plunged in

thought. At last he raised his head, and traces of strong emotion could be seen on his face. 'You have conquered, my friends,' he said sadly.

And, pressing his handkerchief to his face, he left the room with faltering footsteps.

'Badger,' said the Rat, 'I feel like a brute; I wonder what *you* feel like?'

'O, I know, I know,' said the Badger gloomily. 'But the thing had to be done. This good fellow has got to live here, and hold his own, and be respected. Would you have him a common laughing stock, mocked and jeered at by stoats and weasels?'

'Of course not,' said the Rat. 'And, talking of weasels, it's lucky we came upon that little weasel, just as he was setting out with Toad's invitations. I suspected something from what you told me, and had a look at one or two; they were simply disgraceful. I did away with the lot, and the good Mole is now sitting in the blue boudoir, filling up plain, simple invitation cards.'

At last the hour for the banquet began to draw near, and Toad, who on leaving the others had retired to his bedroom, was still

sitting there, sad and thoughtful. His brow resting on his paw, he pondered long and deeply. Gradually his face cleared, and he began to smile long, slow smiles. Then he took to giggling in a shy, self-conscious manner. At last he got up, locked the door, drew the curtains across the windows, collected all the chairs in the room and arranged them in a semicircle, and took up his position in front of then, swelling visibly. Then he bowed, coughed twice, and, letting himself go, with uplifted voice he sang, to the enraptured audience that his imagination so clearly saw –

TOAD'S LAST LITTLE SONG!

The Toad – came – home!
There was panic in the parlour and
howling in the hall,
There was crying in the cowshed and
shrieking in the stall,
When the Toad – came – home!

When the Toad – came – home!
There was smashing in of window and
crashing in of door,
There was chivvying of weasels that
fainted on the floor,
When the Toad – came – home!

Bang! go the drums!
The trumpeters are tooting and the
soldiers are saluting,
And the cannons they are shooting and
the motor-cars are hooting,
As the – Hero – comes!

Shout – Hoo-ray!
And let each one of the crowd try and
shout it very loud,
In honour of an animal of whom you're
justly proud,
For it's Toad's – great – day!

He sang this very loudly, with great energy and expression; and when he had done, he sang it all over again. Then he heaved a deep sigh; a long, long, long sigh.

Then he dipped his hairbrush in the water jug, parted his hair in the middle, and plastered it down very straight and sleek on each side of his face; and, unlocking the door, went quietly down the stairs to greet his guests, who he knew must be assembling in the drawing room.

All the animals cheered when he entered, and crowded round to congratulate him and say nice things about his courage, and his cleverness, and his fighting qualities; but Toad only smiled faintly and murmured, 'Not at all!' Or, sometimes, for a change, 'On the contrary!' The animals were evidently puzzled and taken aback by this unexpected attitude of his; and Toad felt, as he moved from one guest to the other, making his modest responses, that he was an object of great interest to everyone.

The Badger had ordered everything of the best, and the banquet was a great success. There was much talking and laughter among the animals, but through it all Toad, who of course was in the chair, looked down his nose and murmured pleasant nothings to the animals on either side of him. Now and then he stole a glance at the Badger and the Rat, and always when he looked they were staring at each other with their mouths open; and this gave him the greatest satisfaction. Some of the younger and livelier animals, as the evening wore on, got whispering to each other that things were not so amusing as they used to be in the good old days; and there were some knockings on the table and cries of 'Toad! Speech! Speech from Toad! Song! Mr Toad's Song!' But Toad only shook his head gently, raised one paw in mild protest, and managed to convey to them that this dinner was being run on strictly conventional lines.

He was indeed an altered Toad!

After this climax, the four animals continued to lead their lives, so rudely broken in upon by civil war, in great joy and contentment, undisturbed by further risings or invasions. Toad, after due consultation with his friends, selected a handsome gold chain and locket set with pearls, which his dispatched to the gaoler's daughter with a letter that even the Badger admitted to be modest and grateful. The engine-driver, in his turn, was properly thanked and rewarded for all his pains and trouble. Under the strongest pressure from the Badger, even the barge-woman was, with some trouble, sought out and the value of her horse made good to her; though Toad kicked terribly at this. The amount involved, it was true, was not very great.

Sometimes, in the course of long summer evenings, the friends would take a stroll together in the Wild Wood, now successfully tamed so far as they were concerned; and it was pleasing to see how respectfully they were greeted by the inhabitants, and how the mother weasels would bring their young ones to the mouths of their holes, and say, pointing, 'Look, baby! There goes the great Mr Toad! And that's the gallant Water Rat, a terrible fighter, walking along o' him! And yonder comes the famous Mr Mole, of whom you so often have heard your father tell!' But when their infants were troublesome and quite beyond control, they would quiet them by telling how, if they didn't hush themselves and not fret them, the terrible grey Badger would up and get them. This was not true at all of Badger, who, though he cared little about Society, was rather fond of children; but it never failed to have its full effect.